FEATURED ON 20
THE YEAR LISTS IN

"Astonishing... a perfect blend of genres and ideas, and one of the best crime books out there."

– **MATTHEW JACKSON**, *SyFy Wire*

"Nuanced characters, gorgeously mood-setting art, and an impressively layered story... the kind of textured plotting you might expect from Raymond Chandler if he were writing today."

– **DUSTIN NELSON**, *Thrillist*

"A unique blend of old and new which elevates the medium of comics... historical as well as political and touches on hot button topics that are just as important in 2021 as they were in the 1930s."

– **DALTON NORMAN**, *Screenrant*

"Dark and violent and beautiful."

– **JIM DANDENEAU**, *Den of Geek*

"This series — at once historical and timely — teaches as it stings. Its furious didacticism invests the genre's usual damaged, conflicted characters with new meaning. Gripping, nasty, powerful."

– **CHARLES HATFIELD**, *The Comics Journal*

"From top to bottom this book sings: the characters, plot, pencils, layouts, letters, and especially the COLORS! Top it off with the most educational and personal back matter of any book on the stands, and you have one of the best books of 2021."

– **FIRE GUY RYAN**, *ComicTom101*

"One of the best pieces of art in any medium that debuted in 2021. Arguably, it could be the single best comic of the year."

– **HANK REA**, *Lotusland Comics*

"This is the food you eat, which makes you tear up, as you suddenly realize how truly starved you were, and how bad it really was before you got to eat it. We need this. We need more people to read this. It's bloody brilliant."

– **RITESH BABU**, *ComicsXF*

"Dripping with noir-ish style... immediately engaging."

– **AVERY KAPLAN**, *Comics Beat*

"Compelling crime storytelling and stark mirror of the nation's racist legacies... Definitely one of the year's best limited series."

– **PAUL LAI**, *Multiversity Comics*

"Emotionally raw, with complex characters and tough moral quandaries."

– **JOHN MILES**, *Comic Book Resources*

"Impressive... breathe[s] new life into the ground broken by Chandler and Hammett."

– **CHRISTOPHER FARNSWORTH**, *Book and Film Globe*

ADDITIONAL PRAISE

"The gripping story of a detective who knows he'll have to lose a few battles if he's going to win a war."
– **ROB THOMAS** (*Veronica Mars, iZombie* showrunner)

"The best noir comic I've read in years."
– **G. WILLOW WILSON** (*Ms. Marvel, Invisible Kingdom*)

"This is absolutely the best kind of comics noir."
– **KIERON GILLEN** (THE WICKED AND THE DIVINE, DIE)

"Stunning."
– **RAM V.** (*The Many Deaths of Laila Starr, Swamp Thing*)

"Fantastic."
– **JEFF LEMIRE** (GIDEON FALLS, *Sweet Tooth*)

"This is the book I've been waiting for."
– **CLIFF CHIANG** (PAPER GIRLS, *Catwoman: Lonely City*)

"One of the best debuts of the year... ambitious, engrossing, and relevant."
– **BORYS KIT**, *Heat Vision, The Hollywood Reporter*

"Stunning."
– **JOCK** (WYTCHES, *Batman: One Dark Knight*)

"Gorgeous."
– **MATT BAUME**, *The Stranger*

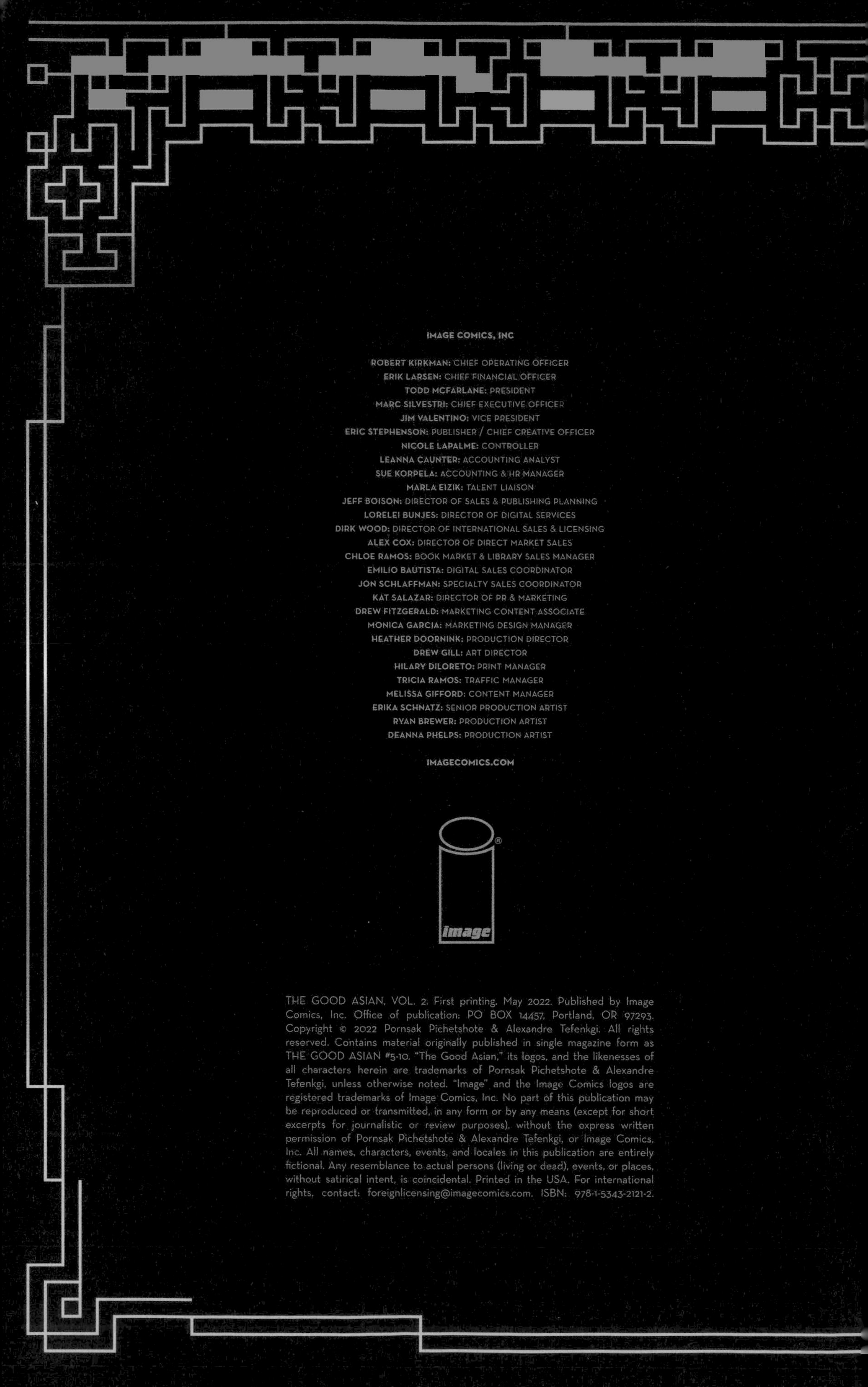

THE GOOD ASIAN, VOL. 2. First printing. May 2022. Published by Image Comics, Inc. Office of publication: PO BOX 14457, Portland, OR 97293.

Printed in the USA. For international rights, contact: foreignlicensing@imagecomics.com. ISBN: 978-1-5343-2121-2.

AN EDISON HARK MYSTERY

PORNSAK PICHETSHOTE
WRITER

ALEXANDRE TEFENKGI
ARTIST

LEE LOUGHRIDGE
COLORIST

JEFF POWELL
LETTERER & DESIGNER

DAVE JOHNSON
COVER ARTIST

GRANT DIN
HISTORICAL CONSULTANT

ERIKA SCHNATZ
LOGO DESIGNER & PRODUCTION

WILL DENNIS
EDITOR

INTRODUCTION

Fuck you chink

Go back to China

Go back to where you came from

I grew up with this

It hurt

It made me feel sad alone like an outsider like I didn't belong

But also a small % of the hurt was because it wasn't even accurate it was lazy if you did a little digging you'd know I was a gook

And if you went even further you'd see I was neither. My oppressors aren't going to take the extra time to get my ethnic background correct but neither did I. I was taught to be less than by outsiders and within my own community and my own family. Why speak up your voice does not matter

Why would I expect my oppressors to look deep when even I didn't look that deep because of laziness? Or something more resembling shame? Who would do the digging to get us those answers?

For anyone not Asian I'll briefly explain Asian culture

It's shut the fuck up and keep your head down, be invisible, you don't matter, the individual does not matter, the family is everything, image and how you make the family look is everything, sacrifice and martyr yourself for everyone but yourself, suffer silently, Never complain, let them curse you, beat you, harass threaten bully beat you down burn your stores, say nothing, smile and take it, take that anger and hatred, bury it deep and use it as revenge fuel, work hard, word harder than anyone and then become rich, own everything and then when you are on top serve the revenge very cold, fire everyone that ever fucked with you punish those who punished you and their entire families. That's why you never hear from us, stealth mode. We never forget. Success is the best revenge, get there quietly without ever complaining.

Art has always been the answer for me, it has saved me and the planet multiple times, it's as important as a doctor or lawyer because it changes culture and perception.

But try telling that to an immigrant parent that art is as important as medicine and law and you get the belt. Which is why Pornsak is an outlier an anomaly a treasure and a gift to me and the culture.

Because you've never heard a voice like his.

THANK GOD FOR PORNSAK, who by all accounts is a "Good Asian" but I see the truth. For Pornsak the writer to exist means he went against his culture, so he's a "Bad Asian."

Bad Asian is what I've been my entire life

Long greasy hair

Heavy metal

Poor grades

Criminal record

No piano

I've been called a Chigger before

So when I saw the title "GOOD ASIAN," I picked it up as a goof.

I looked at my friend Rhode and my brother Paul, what are the chances this is any good I asked.

And I was right... it's not good.

Its fucking great! I love this shit

I'm so happy, I cried.

This fucker this brilliant Pornsak fucker addresses all my baggage and all this heavy cultural shit in a trojan horse of a Chinatown murder mystery.

I learn facts and true shit every issue that I never knew (because once again no talking!)

I've only met Pornsak recently and have only hung out a handful of times, the first time we met, even though we live in Thaitown we didn't just have Thai food, we had northern Thai food from a very specific region, while we were bro'ing out his mom and his sister completely randomly drove an hour in traffic to eat here at the same time, very specific tastes. It runs in the family and this level of attention to detail is what he brings to his writing. This is the shit I love.

For all new Good Asian readers, the complex characters and well-crafted plotlines are self evident...

But Pornsak's incredibly thorough research with the goal of historical accuracy (regardless of the fictional storyline), the importance of not brushing this shameful/overtly-racist period under the metaphorical carpet, and not letting America/Americans remember itself/themselves with bullshit rose-colored glasses.

His level of dedication really shows; even in the post-comic wrap-up section! (if you finish the trade and you love it like I do go back and buy the individual issues, because there's so much great extra stuff in the letters column and the interviews in the back pages of the individual issues).

Alexandre Tefenkgi's art is solid. Initially, his style struck me as simplistic/minimal, but over time I found it deceptive because he fills the panels with mad nuance and subtlety. His artwork is a great match and complements the story very well. (Also big-up to Lee Loughridge's color work!)

I'm not an actor but the only reason I agreed to write this intro is so I can finally play a good Asian on the big screen when you know Hollywood eventually turns this into a movie.

The book is beautiful.

It's better than a movie. It's thrilling and makes you think and it's fun and entertaining.

But more than that

It's important and it matters

And it's brave enough to explore the question

Go back to where you come from

David Choe
2/2/22 Northern Thai Food Club

Long famous for his fine art which has garnered the respect and adulation of museums and fans around the world, iconoclastic painter David Choe is one of the few fine artists to successfully jump from the museum to the media world. Dubbed "the prince of all media" by Howard Stern, Choe has directed well-regarded music videos and has had his art featured on multi-platinum album covers. In 2021, his television show The Choe Show *premiered on FX.*

PREVIOUSLY...
IT'S 1936, AND...

THE CARROWAY FAMILY

EDISON HARK is one of America's first Chinese-American detectives, belonging to a generation of Chinese Americans growing up under the Chinese Exclusion Act, an immigration law prohibiting scores of Chinese from entering America.

Sugar tycoon **MASON CARROWAY** raised Hark like a surrogate son in his Hawaii home before the rest of the family moved to San Francisco. Mason is currently in a coma.

FRANKIE CARROWAY. Mason's eldest, summoned Edison to San Francisco to find the missing woman his father loves. Frankie was just murdered trying to help Hark.

VICTORIA CARROWAY, Mason's youngest, hasn't seen Edison since they were children, one of many secrets from their complicated past.

IVY CHEN, Mason's love (and maid) went missing after the two fought. Frankie believed the resulting heartbreak triggered his father's coma and sent for Hark to find her.

THE CHINATOWN PLAYERS

Ivy's trail overlapped with **HUI LONG** – a masked Tong assassin settling old scores. Hark discovered the killer was in fact *white*, moments before he murdered Frankie.

Local lawyer **TERENCE CHENG** – Chinatown's "Great Yellow Hope" – has brought the Carroways and other investors to fund local Chinatown businesses, bolstering the economy. He was attacked by Hui Long at a local night club.

BENNIE AND DONNIE YAN own **THE JADE CASTLE** – the night club where Hui Long attempted to murder Terence, only to accidentally kill Bennie instead.

DETECTIVE O'MALLEY is an old-school Irish cop in San Francisco's Chinatown Squad. The racist cop carries a grudge against Hark.

OTHER CHINATOWN FACES

Chinatown telephone operator **LUCY FAN** was helping Hark before rejecting him upon learning of his problematic nature. The two had a mutual friend in Hawaii resident Wilbur Manalao.

Lucy's friend **TONY ZHAO** almost stabbed Hark — retaliation for Hark violently arresting Tony's father for opium possession.

HELEN CHAO — the sister of Ivy's dead best friend and potential accomplice **HOLLY** — found proof her sister (and perhaps Ivy) was blackmailing Terence Chang.

*TRANSLATED FROM CANTONESE.

CHAPTER FIVE

ART BY **DAVE JOHNSON**

ART BY **AFU CHAN**

HOLY COW...
YOU DREW THAT?

HEY, I'M FRANKIE...
YOU'RE THE MAID'S SON, RIGHT?
THE ONE NAMED AFTER THE INVENTOR...
EDISON!

CAN I CALL YOU EDDY?
UM, SURE... YOU--YOU WANT TO DRAW TOO?
I'VE GOT EXTRA PENCILS.
NO WAY-- I'LL NEVER BE AS GOOD AS YOU.

I MEAN, I BETCHA YOU'LL BE A FAMOUS ARTIST SOMEDAY.
I BET!

HIS EYEBALL BURST?
YEAH. IT...
...IT WAS THE USUAL GAG--DRESS LIKE A SEE YUP GUY--
"SNEAK IN, SELL STUFF--GET A GANDER ON THE OPERATION--
"BUT TSCHUN KWONG FINGERED ME BEFORE THE FLATFOOTS STORMED IN.
"SO...BRIGHT SIDE? THE SQUAD SHUT DOWN HONOLULU'S BIGGEST GAMBLING RING.
"BUT NOW THE WORD'S OUT. EVERY CROOK'LL SEE ME COMING. NO MORE SNEAKING IN ANYWHERE.
"PLUS, IN ORDER TO GET TSCHUN KWONG OFF ME--
CRACK
"...I HEARD HE'S HALF-BLIND NOW."

BOY, STOP BEIN' GLUM. YOU JUST BEEN PROMOTED TO DETECTIVE. SO YOU LOST YOUR-- WHATZZIT--"COVER"--
WILBUR...I BECAME A COP 'CUZ I WANTED ONE THAT ORIENTALS FELT SAFE AROUND, AND NOW...
...YOU SAW WHAT HAPPENED TO CHANG APANA. THEY BASED THAT CHARLIE CHAN MOVIE AFTER HIM!
BUT IF EVERYONE'LL SEE YOU COMIN'...
BE THE BRIDGE. SHOW AMERICANS THEY CAN TRUST ORIENTALS.
'CUZ YOU AND ME BOTH KNOW--
IF WE WANT HAOLES TO TRUST US LOCALS-- TO TREAT US EVEN CLOSE TO HOW THEY TREAT EACH OTHER?
DETECTIVE
WE GOTTA PLAY BY THEIR RULES...
WE GOTTA BE UNDENIABLE.
"WHAT ARE YOU DOING? HUH?!"

FRANKIE'S BY HIMSELF! AND YOU'RE HERE... DRAWING??
OW!

MA, I'M ALWAYS WITH FRANKIE--! WHY CAN'T I DRAW WITH MY OTHER FRIENDS --

WHEN YOU'RE IN TROUBLE, YOU THINK DRAWING WILL HELP? OR THOSE FRIENDS?

EDISON, DO YOU REMEMBER WHY YOUR BABA LEFT?
DO YOU?

YEAH...

BECAUSE YOUR FATHER LOST EVERYTHING ON PAI GOW. AND WHEN THEY CAME TO COLLECT, WHAT HAPPENED?
HE--HE LEFT--

HE RAN BACK TO CHINA!
AND DID ANY CHINESE HERE HELP US? HUH? COULD THEY?

NO. IF MASON CARROWAY HADN'T TAKEN PITY--GIVEN ME A JOB, WE'D STILL BE PAYING BACK YOUR BABA'S DEBT.

BUT YOU HAVE WHAT NEITHER ME OR YOUR FATHER DID.
AN AMERICAN LIKES YOU!

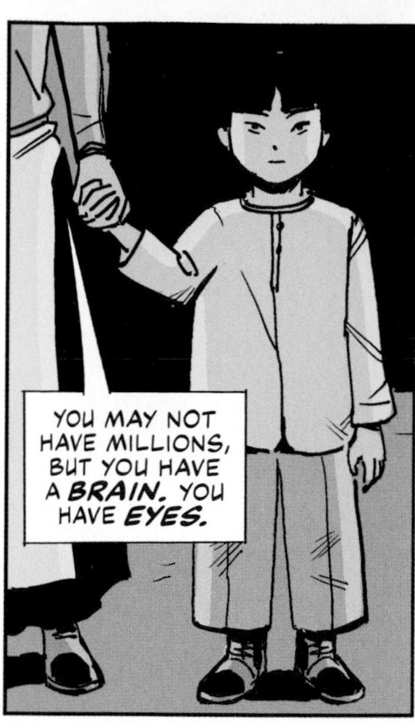

"YOU **PAY ATTENTION.** WHEN THEY'RE **NERVOUS.** WHEN THEY'RE **RELIEVED.** ALL THE DIFFERENT WAYS THEY THINK THE WORLD OWES THEM **HAPPINESS.** THEY'LL TELL YOU **EVERYTHING** ABOUT HOW THEY WANT TO BE TREATED. YOU JUST HAVE TO **PAY ATTENTION.**"

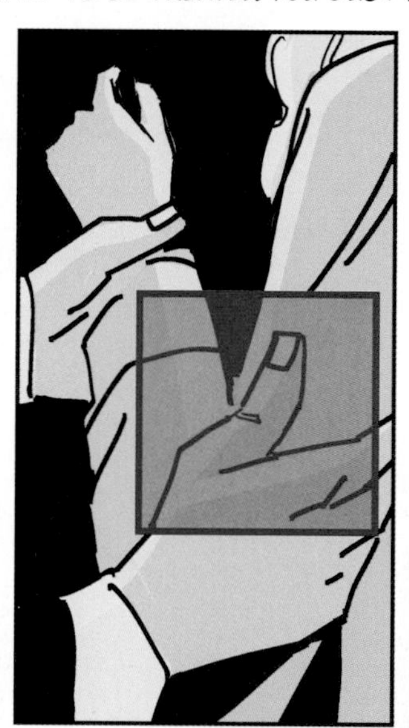

EDISON...
YOU--YOU SHOULDN'T BE HERE...
...AFTER EVERYTHING SHE DID FOR US...IF ANYTHING EVER HAPPENED, I PROMISED YOUR MOTHER, EDISON--
--I'D RAISE YOU LIKE YOU WERE MINE.
THIS...IS FOR ME?
BUT I--I THOUGHT I'D--I'D SLEEP IN MY--

THIS IS YOUR ROOM NOW.
I OWE YOU--YOUR MOTHER...
SHE SAID THE BOLTS ON THE DOOR WEREN'T LOCKING, BUT I...

WE'RE GOING TO FIND THE BASTARD WHO DID IT.
I SWEAR ON EVERYTHING HOLY--
FATHER!

VICTORIA?!
FRANKIE RUINED MY--
I TRIED STOPPING HER, FATHER. BUT DADDY'S PRINCESS THOUGHT--

I SAID I NEEDED TO SPEAK WITH EDISON. ALONE.
BUT FATHER, FRANKIE RIPPED--

I DON'T CARE.
BOTH OF YOU RETURN TO YOUR ROOMS. THIS INSTANT.

WE'LL SPEAK OF YOUR PUNISHMENTS FOR INTERRUPTING US LATER.
"I KNOW WHAT I'M DOING--"

LOOK, MR. CARROWAY ASKED ME TO HELP YOU BEFORE WE POSED FOR OUR SUMMER PICTURE--
OH, AND GOD **FORBID** YOU NOT PROVE YOU'RE SMARTER THAN ME--

YEP. **THIS** IS GOING PREDICTABLY BAD.
YOU THINK YOU HAVE EVERYONE FOOLED. THAT YOU'RE SOME **ANGELIC CREATURE.**

BUT I **SEE** YOU--
OBSEQUIOUS TO **FRANKIE.** TO **FATHER.**
SO DESPERATE FOR THEIR ACCEPTANCE.

SO TERRIFIED FATHER'S CHARITY WILL DRY OUT--
YEP. **PREDICTABLY** BA--

FATHER...?
MR. CARROWAY!

FATHER!

...YES, FRANKIE'S HEADING OVER FROM A FRIEND'S.

WILL FATHER... BE ALL RIGHT?
WE NEED MORE TESTS. YOUR FATHER'S GENERAL HEALTH IS FINE, BUT...

...HE WAS BORN WITH A *WEAK HEART.*

WITH ALL DUE RESPECT, DOCTOR--

--ONLY A *FOOL* DOUBTS MASON CARROWAY'S *HEART.*
"I'M TELLING YOU, SHE'LL *BE* AT THE PARTY...."

WHO SAYS THAT?

EVERYBODY.

THEY SAY NO ONE'S GOOD ENOUGH FOR EDISON HARK...

...THE CARROWAY COMMUNITY SCHOOL IS FATHER'S BIGGEST CONTRIBUTION TO THE CITY.
AND HE PUT YOU IN CHARGE OF THE OPENING, BECAUSE HE TRUSTS YOU MORE THAN ANY OF US.
NOT BECAUSE IT'S A SCHOOL FOR CHINATOWN KIDS.
BOTH THESE THINGS CAN BE TRUE.
GOD, AT THIS RATE, I'D BE SHOCKED IF YOU DON'T END UP HEADING THE COMPANY ONE DAY.
AS IF WE BOTH DON'T KNOW YOU'RE RUNNING IT.
WE KNOW NO SUCH THING. FATHER DOESN'T THINK A WOMAN'S UP TO THE JOB, REMEMBER?
HE NEVER SAID--
THEN YOU HAVEN'T BEEN LISTENING.
FROM THE MINUTE I WAS BORN, HE'S TALKED ABOUT THE CARROWAY RESPONSIBILITY TO ENSURE EVERY MAN IS TREATED EQUAL.
EVERY MAN.
THE GREAT MASON CARROWAY IS MANY THINGS. INCLUDING A HYPOCRITE.
THE COMPANY'S NOT GOING TO ME.
SO...WHO?
FRANKIE...?

NAAAAHHHHHH...
THAT'S SO MEAN.
GOD, I HATE LYING TO HIM--
WELL, FRANKIE'S A GOSSIP, AND YOU'RE SO WORRIED ABOUT PEOPLE FINDING US OUT--
WE GREW UP TOGETHER AND NOW WE'RE--
UH, NO...I'VE SPENT TEN YEARS AT ST. THERESA'S PREPARATORY IN SAN FRANCISCO--
I'M HOME SUMMERS. I'M NOT ASHAMED OF--
OF SLEEPING AROUND IN A FIELD HAND'S ABANDONED HUT? YOU SHOULD BE--
EDISON...MY ENTIRE LIFE--I'VE BEEN FOCUSED ON WHAT'S NEXT. THE NEXT ACCOMPLISHMENT. THE NEXT ACHIEVEMENT.
BUT WHEN I'M WITH YOU...
I'M NOT THINKING ABOUT WHAT'S NEXT. I'M JUST...
I'M HAPPY I'M HERE.
...
ME TOO.
EDDY... I...
I'M LATE.
LATE...? LATE FOR--?
OH.

...I--I DON'T KNOW WHERE IT *WENT...*I PUT THE GUEST LIST RIGHT--

I'M LATE.

EDISON.
ORGANIZING THE SCHOOL OPENING IS A LARGE RESPONSIBILITY FOR SOMEONE YOUR AGE, BUT MY FATHER...
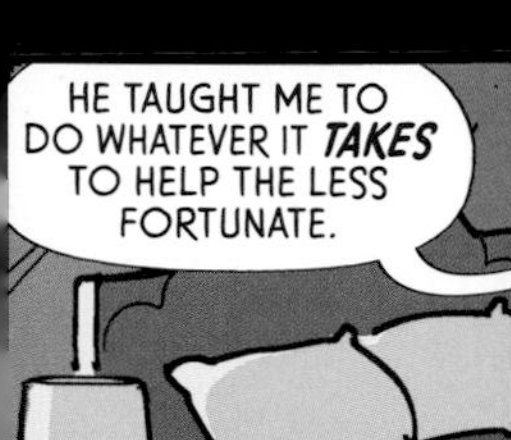
HE TAUGHT ME TO DO WHATEVER IT *TAKES* TO HELP THE LESS FORTUNATE.

BUT ALL MY CHARITIES CAN DO IS *HELP* OTHER PEOPLE CHANGE THINGS.
PEOPLE LIKE *YOU* CAN MAKE THEM BETTER.
ME? HOW--?
YOU'LL ACCOMPLISH MORE IN YOUR LIFE THAN *I* EVER WILL.

YOU'RE NOT *SPOILED.*

NOT LIKE *MY* CHILDREN.

YOU WON'T SQUANDER *ANY* OF THIS.

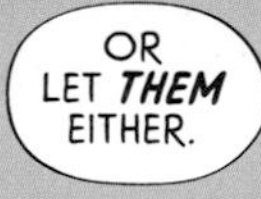
OR LET *THEM* EITHER.

THAT'S WHY I *TRUST* YOU.

WHAT DO YOU MEAN--YOU'RE NOT COMING TO SAN FRANCISCO?
WHEN WE STARTED THIS-- WE KNEW IT WOULDN'T LAST--
AND IN THE PAST THREE YEARS--
WE PROVED WE WERE WRONG--
HOLD ON-- DID YOU ORGANIZE ALL THIS TO... BREAK UP?
BECAUSE... ONE DAY, YOU'LL BE MARRIED. TO SOMEONE ELSE.
AND I'LL HAVE TO WATCH IT HAPPEN--
EDISON, NO...
FINE... IF YOU WON'T GO, NEITHER WILL I.
VICTORIA, YOU'RE NOT GIVING UP RUNNING THE FAMILY COMPANY. MASON'D NEVER FORGIVE ME IF I RUINED YOUR LIFE.

EDISON, I KNOW THE IDEA OF US...WITH CHILD WAS ALARMING--BUT IT WAS A FALSE ALARM--
I KNOW IT'S HARD IN HONOLULU WHERE EVERYONE KNOWS US.
THEN WHAT THE HELL IS IT?!
BUT IN THE CITY, WE CAN RE-TEACH PEOPLE WHO WE ARE--
IT'S NOT THAT--
IT'S ABOUT CALIFORNIA NOT BEING HAWAII. INTERMARRIAGE'S ILLEGAL THERE. WE KNOW THAT--
AND I DON'T CARE.
AND I HAVE TO.
WHAT? FATHER THINKS THE WORLD OF--
"THE GREAT MASON CARROWAY IS MANY THINGS. INCLUDING A HYPOCRITE," REMEMBER?
THAT-- THAT'S NOT WHAT I MEANT...
IT DOESN'T MATTER. YOU CAN'T MAKE ME GO.
I'M STAYING.
FINE...

"...THEN SO AM *I.*"
PLEASE, EDDY. I DIDN'T DO IT! PLEASE...
WILBUR...I DON'T KNOW WHAT YOU ***HEARD,*** BUT I'M ***SURE*** YOU HEARD IT WRONG.
THAT MOVIE STAR--HE SAID I ***FORCED MYSELF*** ON HIS WIFE??
OK, MAYBE NOT SO WRONG.
I DIDN'T DO IT!
OF ***COURSE*** YOU DIDN'T. THAT'S WHY ***I'M*** HERE.
SO WE CAN ***WALK*** INTO THAT STATION AND ***PROVE*** YOU'VE NOTHING TO BE SCARED OF.
WHEN'S ANYONE EVER BELIEVED A ***FILIPINO*** OVER A *HAOLE?*
YOU'RE MY ***FRIEND.*** I CAN ***VOUCH--***
IT DOESN'T MATTER. YOU ***READ*** THE PAPERS! THEY'RE THROWING US OFF BRIDGES NOW!
THAT'S CALIFORNIA...

COME ON, WHAT ELSE CAN YOU DO? GO ON THE RUN?
THAT ACTOR... HE'S FAMOUS ENOUGH THAT THE COPS WON'T STOP 'TIL THEY FIND YOU.
BELIEVE ME--I KNOW HOW THIS WORKS.
REMEMBER WHY YOU TOLD ME YOU MOVED HERE FROM SAN FRANCISCO?
YOU SAID YOU WANTED YOUR NEPHEWS TO KNOW THEIR UNCLE.
THE SECOND YOU LEAVE, YOU'RE LOOKING OVER YOUR SHOULDER FOR THE REST OF YOUR LIFE.
LET ME TAKE YOU IN UNTIL THEY FIND THE REAL CULPRIT.
YOU TOLD ME ONCE, WILBUR--
IF WE WANT HAOLES TO TRUST US LOCALS, WE HAVE TO PLAY BY THEIR RULES...
WE HAVE TO BE UNDENIABLE.

MISS...
MISS CARROWAY?
EDISON, WHAT-- WHAT IS ***SHE*** DOING HERE?
GET THE ***FUCK*** OUT.
NOW.
I'M-- I'M SORRY... I DIDN'T WANT YOU FINDING OUT LIKE--
YOU FUCKING COWARD.
YOU'RE GOING TO ***FORCE*** ME TO GO, *HUH?*
IS THAT IT?

LISTEN, I--

...

...EVERYTHING HAPPENED SO ***QUICKLY.*** IT'S NOT YOU, IT'S--

STOP LYING!

STOP.. FUCKING...

EDDY...?

"YEAH, FATHER FOUND VICTORIA'S NOTE. I DON'T UNDERSTAND AT ALL..."
WHAT'S *SHE* SO HOT AND BOTHERED ABOUT?
...WE'RE *ALL* MOVING TO SAN FRANCISCO IN A FEW *WEEKS.*
"SHE DIDN'T SAY ANYTHING TO YOU EITHER?"
WESTERN UNION TELEGRAM
PLEASE EDDY COME TO SAN FRANCISCO FATHER TAKEN ILL WE NEED YOUR HELP
DETECTIVE HARK--!
HM?
DETECTIVE... WE'RE SO SORRY TO HEAR ABOUT YOUR FRIEND--
WILBUR?
I WAS JUST HEADING TO HIS CELL. WHAT'S *WRONG?*
YOU...DON'T KNOW? *UH,* SORRY. WE--WE THOUGHT YOU *KNEW--*

WHAT HAPPENED TO WILBUR?
DETECTIVE, HE--
THAT MOVIE STAR--HE HAD **FANS** IN THE CLINK, AND ONE OF THEM...
WILBUR'S **DEAD,** DETECTIVE.
Come on.
Come **on...**
Head in the **game.**

Promised Frankie... no one else hurt, but...
FRANKIE, I'M SORRY...
He's dead

They'll be
Here soon
COPS...
Tear Chinatown apart looking for Hui Long

'Cuz this time he killed
AMERICAN MILLIONAIRE... BUT...
I can tell them...
Hui Long's...not Chinese. He's white. I can stop this.

As long as they believe
An out-of-town Chink

Just trust the system
Promised Frankie...

follow the
rules

Make sure no one finds **Frankie's body.**

Catch Hui Long before anyone knows Frankie died here.

Be fast, be quiet--

Be perfect--

FUCK!

CHAPTER SIX

ART BY **DAVE JOHNSON**

ART BY **DAVID CHOE**

AHH!
YOU SICK--
I remember O'Malley, and then...
!
Pieces.

AHH--!
UHH!!
Dammit--
Re-opened my wound--
Gotta end this before he--
Notices.
YOU FUCK--
YOU WANNA PLAY SICK GAMES?
WHAT--?!
HAHH?!
AAAHHHH!!

AH!
BHPPP
GHHHAAA
SPIT
YOU...
YOU FUCKING--
ANIMA--
AHH!
THDD
THDD
THDD
THD
Moving
Moving Frankie doesn't make sense anymore
PANT
PANT
...NNN...
...gotta just bite the bullet...

...OUR DETECTIVE SUSPECTED THE JADE CASTLE WAS HOLDING BACK ON US SO HE CIRCLED AROUND TO INQUIRE. CAUGHT HARK IN THE ACT.
SFPD
DON'T WORRY, MS. CARROWAY-- WE FOUND HIS VEHICLE 'CROSS TOWN-- TIRE BLOWN OUT.
BUT WE'LL POST A CAR OUT FRONT, JUST IN CASE.
YOU'RE LUCKY YOU'RE HERE AND NOT IN THE CITY.
I--I JUST ARRIVED...
MA'AM, WERE YOU AND HARK CLOSE?
...HARDLY.
EDISON NEVER IMPRESSED ME THE WAY HE DID MY FAMILY.
WELL, TRY NOT TO WORRY...
"...IT'S ONLY A MATTER OF TIME 'TIL HE'S CAUGHT."
IT SEEMS YOUR TRICK WORKED...

SLASHING YOUR **OWN** TIRE HAS THEM RUNNING IN THE WRONG DIRECTION.
THEY'VE **NO** IDEA YOU CALLED ME FOR HELP--
AND IF THEY'RE-- *NNN*--
HUNTING **ME,** THEY'VE LESS REASON TO TERRORIZE INNOCENT ORIENTALS.
NOT THAT THEY WON'T ***ANYWAY.***

SO...***SIT DOWN.*** YOUR WOUND NEEDS CHANGING ***ALREADY.***
THE HELP STAY IN A SEPARATE ***BUILDING.*** THEY WON'T BOTHER US.
PLEASE--COME THE MORNING YOU CAN HIDE IN MY TRUNK AGAIN, AND WE'LL DRIVE PAST THE POLICE'S GUARD. ***THEN*** WE'LL FIND FRANKIE'S KILLER.

EDISON...
?

I...
I NEEDED HIM OFF-BALANCE... FRANKIE...

I *KILLED* HIM, VICTORIA.

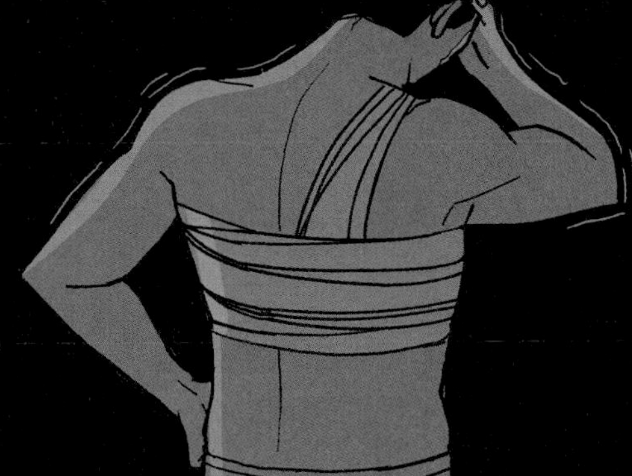

NO...
I--I THOUGHT HE WAS HOLDING BACK AND...

I JUST KEPT PUSHING...
AND *PUSHING...*

I NEEDED HIM...

I NEEDED HIM SLOPPY.

*Victoria's been telling me a story. Of when Mason once offered Ivy a gift--an expensive necklace. And the picture she paints is interesting--of an Ivy Chen **in** over her **head.***

With a job she liked too much to break an old man's heart.

*But Victoria says she also **kept the necklace.** One of possibly **many** keepsakes from Mason. And that certainly fits Ivy's past of wrapping men around her little finger.*

*All interesting nuggets next to the four dead bodies left behind by a **white man** masquerading as a **hatchetman.***

*And while a killer **could've** been hired to give Chinatown and the Tongs a black rap...*

WHY NOT JUST HIRE AN ORIENTAL? WHY GET A GWEILO WHO KNOWS CHINESE MARTIAL ARTS?
'CUZ THIS GUY DEFINITELY DID.
PLUS, "HUI LONG" TARGETED TERENCE CHANG 'CUZ OF HIS LINK TO THE BING HIP TONG. BENNIE AND DONNIE YAN'VE GOT NO LINK--
BUT WASN'T BENNIE'S DEATH ACCIDENTAL--
WAS IT?
TERENCE WAS ATTACKED BEFORE A PACKED HOUSE. GETTING THAT CLOSE TOOK PLANNING.
AND I WAS IN THE BACK ALLEY HE PARKS IN. IT'S GOT NO OVER-LOOKING WINDOWS. WHY RUB HIM OUT WITH AN AUDIENCE WHEN YOU COULD JUST DO IT THERE?
ESPECIALLY WHEN THE REST OF YOUR KILLS WERE IN PRIVATE? UNLESS...
HE WANTED TO BE SEEN "ACCIDENTALLY" SKUNKING BENNIE.
BUT WHY?
YOUR TURN. WHY'D YOU THINK IVY WAS RUNNING FROM MASON?
AND WHAT'S IT GOT TO DO WITH MY MA?

I'M NOT SURE, BUT...
YOU LIONIZED FATHER, BUT HIS WHOLE LIFE--IF HE THOUGHT IT WAS RIGHT, HE'D...CUT CORNERS, DISREGARD THE LAW...
THE LAST TIME IVY AND I SPOKE, I REALIZED FATHER WAS CONFIDING IN HER ON TOPICS HE NEVER MENTIONED TO ME.
HE WAS QUIETLY PAYING A RANSOM.
SO I KEPT REVIEWING OUR BOOKS.
THERE ARE THOUSANDS UNACCOUNTED FOR. HE WITHDREW THEM EVERY THIRD OF THE MONTH--GOING BACK MONTHS.
EVERY...?
I THINK HE WAS BEING BLACK-MAILED.
AND WHEN IVY WASN'T RETURNED, HIS HEART GAVE OUT.
BECAUSE EDISON--THE LONGER I LOOK AT THE HISTORY OF FATHER'S BUSINESS...

SHE DISAPPEARED BEFORE I COULD LEARN EXACTLY HOW MUCH.
YOU FIGURE SHE WAS SNATCHED FOR SOMETHING SHE KNEW?
PERHAPS. AFTER FATHER'S HEART ATTACK, I STARTED REVIEWING OUR FINANCES. HIS RECENT INVESTMENTS IN CHINATOWN WERE HIS MOST AMBITIOUS PHILANTHROPY EVER.
AND THEN THERE'S THE THOUSANDS HE KEEPS IN OUR LOCKBOXES-- IN JEWELRY, BONDS, LOOSE CASH--
WHICH WERE RECENTLY CLEARED OUT. THE BANK MANAGER SAID FATHER VISITED AFTER IVY'S DISAPPEARANCE, ALMOST AS IF...
THE MORE I HAVE TO RE-EXAMINE THE REASONS BEHIND EVERYTHING THAT'S HAPPENED IN OUR LIVES.
And how does all this relate to Ivy Chen?
To Victoria, she's a victim. Of both Mason's transgressions and blackmail.
To me, she's more like a blackmailer getting what's coming to her. An opportunist with her sights on Mason.
Question is, who's right?

...WE'RE ALL MOVING TO SAN FRANCISCO IN A FEW WEEKS. WHY WOULD VICTORIA FLY OUT EARLY?
OR... WHAT? YOU HAD A--A THING FOR MA? HUH??
SHE USEDTA WET YOUR WHISTLE--
DON'T YOU DARE--
WAK
I DIDN'T MEAN TO...
YOU-- YOU OK? FATHER TOLD ME--
SHIT.
HE REALLY HIT YOU??
IT WASN'T HIS FAULT. I WAS PUSHING...

EDDY...YOU DON'T HAVE TO DO THAT. HE'S NOT ***ALWAYS*** RIGHT.
SOMETIMES YOU HAVE TO STAND ***UP*** TO HIM LIKE ***ME--***
BUT I'LL ***NEVER*** BE ***YOU.*** YOU GET THAT, ***RIGHT?***
LOOKING AT US, NO ONE'S ***EVER*** SEEING TWO CARROWAYS.
JUST YOU-- AND YOUR ***COOLIE*** SIDEKICK.

AND NOW... WHOEVER "HUI LONG" IS, HE'S GOT SOMETHING TO DO WITH IVY. AND EVEN IF HE DIDN'T...I HAVE TO CATCH THIS GUY.
FOR FRANKIE.
FOR... FRANKIE?
THE POLICE ARE TERRORIZING CHINATOWN RIGHT NOW, AND YOU HAVE TO CATCH HIM FOR FRANKIE?!
CHRIST, WHEN DOES IT END? WHEN DO YOU STOP DOING THINGS FOR THE...THE RICH GWEILOS IN YOUR LIFE?
SAID THE GWEILO.
NOTHING'S CHANGED, HAS IT? EVERY TIME I FORGET, YOU REMIND ME...
SOME NIGHTS--WE'D BE IN BED--AND IT WAS LIKE I COULD HEAR YOUR HEART--
AND HOW MUCH IT HATED THIS BODY IT WAS IN.
THIS BODY I LOVED.
AND I TOLD MYSELF I'D DO ANYTHING TO STOP THAT.
AND I ONLY REALIZED I COULDN'T THE NIGHT I FOUND YOU WITH THAT GIRL.

BECAUSE YOU'D RATHER BELIEVE THINGS CAN'T CHANGE. BECAUSE OF WHAT YOU'D HAVE TO GIVE UP IF THEY DID.
LET ME GUESS.
NOW THAT YOU RUN MASON'S COMPANY--
NOW THAT YOU GOT YOUR BOARD TO RESPECT THEIR LADY BOSS, YOU GET WHAT I GO THROUGH?
I'M SAYING, YOU STARTED HATING YOURSELF LONG BEFORE YOU MET MY FAMILY.
LOOK...THE POLICE ARE HUNTING YOU. YOU'LL HAVE TO HIDE IN MY TRUNK AGAIN JUST TO GET PAST THEIR GUARD OUTSIDE.
SO JUST TELL ME WHAT ELSE YOU NEED.
A CAR? A GUN?
...
A PENCIL.

The late Holly Chao was Ivy's best friend--and potential accomplice. When Lucy and I spoke with her sister Helen, she mentioned Holly ran with a lot of gweilos.
YEAH...HE WAS WITH HOLLY A LOT. HE DIDN'T HAVE THOSE SCARS, THOUGH...
Holly bragged he was the illegitimate heir of Abraham Woodward. Of course, her sister dismissed it.
Victoria pretended I told Holly's family about them before I disappeared...
And while Victoria worried they wouldn't talk to this spoiled rich lady just showing up--
I've wagered more on less.
One of San Francisco's richest, most powerful women--
Offers them a way their daughter's senseless death could help the very public murder of her brother...
They'd do everything they could...
Even if Victoria wasn't offering to pay for Holly's funeral.

Victoria tells me Abraham Woodward was a millionaire with factories across the state.
One of them manufactured paint and closed down with the Depression.
And I recognized the scars on "Hui Long"'s face...
Chemical burns.
TAKE IT. I STILL CAN'T BELIEVE YOU'RE NOT CARRYING ONE.
EVEN IF I COULD HAVE BROUGHT IT TO THE MAINLAND--
FLATFOOTS TEND TO SHOOT FIRST WHEN THEY SEE ARMED CHINAMEN.
Except now...
Now everyone's shooting first.
YOU KNOW... I THOUGHT IT'D BE HARDER.
?
TO CONVINCE YOU FATHER MIGHT BE BREAKING THE LAW.

I think about finally saying it. Out loud to someone else. About **Michael Martinez**--the man who killed my mother.

But instead...

I say the only thing I **know's** true.

The fact Holly's sister recognized "Hui Long" **without** his burns means they're relatively **recent.**
So if this factory **was** where he got burned, **some** trace of that visit might still be around.
Because **stopping** Hui Long, finding **some** proof **tying** him to the killings, **that's** the only prayer I've got to stop the Blues from waging war on Chinatown and clear my name.
Unfortunately, if Hui Long **is** targeting Terence, **he's** moving as fast as **I** am.
'Cuz--like me--he's got **no choice.** The window to get at Terence is closing too **fast** for him to stay in any one place. Making him long **gone** by--
FLAMMABLE LIQUID
3

LOOK WHO WE HAVE HERE...
SOMEONE TO PLAY WITH...

YOU'RE WORKING FOR THEM, AREN'T YOU?

WHY WOULD YOU *HELP* THEM? YOU SHOULD BE ON *OUR* SIDE--

"HUI LONG"-- WHO--WHOEVER YOU ARE...

IT-- IT WON'T WORK...

kak kak

ALL THIS *KILLING* WON'T BRING HER BACK--

IT WON'T... BRING IVY CHEN BACK...

SUNLIGHT PAINT

BEST PAINT IN THE WORLD

YOU-- YOU WERE RIGHT. I **WAS** A FOOL...
YES. I LEFT HIM AT THE OLD WOODWARD FACTORY.
JUST... GET THERE QUICKLY...
PLEASE, MR. NASH--
THIS ALL HAS TO END.

CHAPTER SEVEN

ART BY **DAVE JOHNSON**

ART BY **SONGMUANG CHUAYNUKOON**

MOTHER, PLEASE...IF WE HAD ANYONE ELSE TO ASK--

NO. YOU HAD THE OPPORTUNITY FOR YOUR FATHER AND I TO BE PART OF YOUR LIFE--

MOTHER...IT'S JUN'S HEART. WITHOUT THE SURGERY, HE'LL--HE'LL...

YOU TURNED YOUR BACK ON US--ON THE WOODWARD NAME--

WE'LL PAY YOU BACK, ALL RIGHT?! PLEASE! JUST...

DO IT FOR SILAS. YOUR GRANDSON.
WITHOUT THIS OPERATION...
HIS FATHER WILL DIE.

AND...YOU AND DADDY CAN BE PART OF OUR LIVES NOW. YOU CAN SEE SILAS WHENEVER YOU'D LIKE, OK?

HE--HE DOESN'T EVEN LOOK...THAT... ORIENTAL...

SLAM

Shot in my **stabbed** shoulder.

Barely feel my arm...

WHAT DID THEY DO TO *IVY?!* WHAT DID THE *CARROWAYS--*

SHE'S MY *SISTER!*

MY SISTER!!

Right...

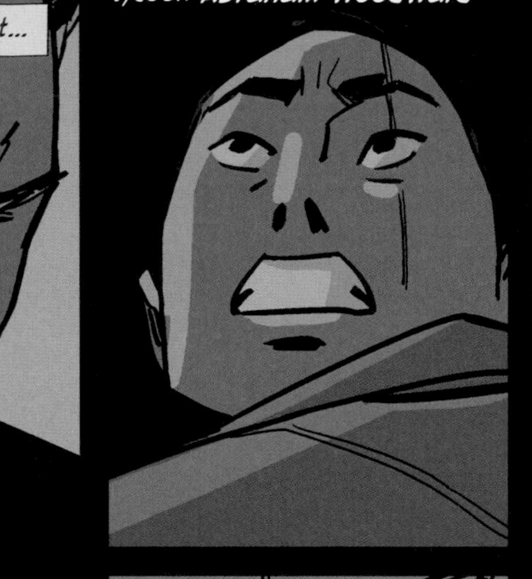

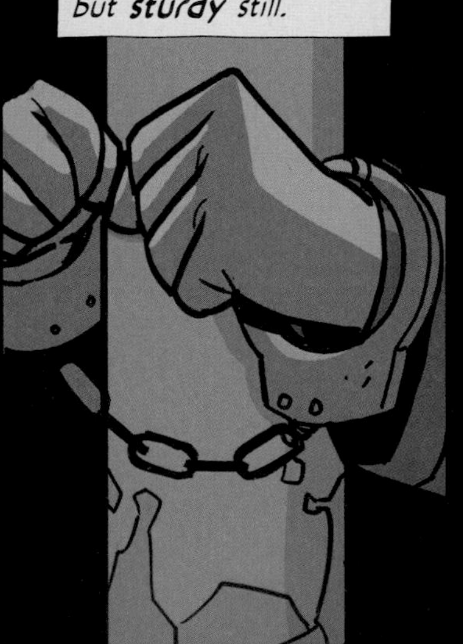

Think... Stall...
I KNOW... IF YOU'RE LOOKING FOR REVENGE... A BLOODTHIRSTY HATCHETMAN'S A NICE SMOKE SCREEN.

"IVY... MUST HAVE TOLD YOU ABOUT HUI LONG... BASED ON STORIES SHE HEARD GROWING UP FROM THE CHATTY BOOTLEGGER IN HER BUILDING.
TALKED TO EVERY-BODY--HE ALWAYS HAD A STORY--

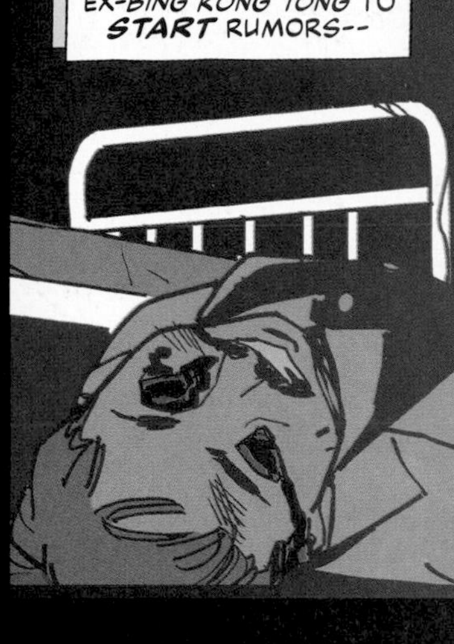
"SO YOU KILLED AN EX-BING KONG TONG TO START RUMORS--

"THEN THE OLD BOOTLEGGER HIMSELF TO COVER THE TRACKS. RIGHT?

"ALL TO HIDE WHO YOU REALLY WANTED DEAD... BY PRETENDING TO BE A CHINESE KILLER."

COME ON, BETWEEN US, WE CAN FIND IVY...

If I don't get out of these cuffs first--
Snap your goddamn neck--

WHY WOULD YOU WORK FOR THEM...?
YOU'RE CHINESE! WHY WOULD YOU WORK FOR THEM?!

WHAT DID MASON DO? HUH?
WHATEVER IT IS, I WON'T LET HIM GET AWAY WITH IT.

YOU WON'T--?
YOU?? YOU'RE THEIR COOLIE.
THEY PROBABLY DIDN'T EVEN NEED TO PROMISE YOU ANYTHING.
I BET JUST THE IDEA WAS ENOUGH.
OF EATING AT THEIR TABLE.
THEM SAYING YOUR NAME RIGHT.
BUT, YOU MUST KNOW--YOU'RE SMART ENOUGH--
THEY'LL NEVER REALLY SEE YOU--
HEY...WHATEVER MASON DID. HE WON'T GET AWAY WITH IT. OK?
EVEN VICTORIA-- HIS OWN DAUGHTER-- SHE'S--
UHHH!!
DON'T YOU SAY THAT NAME!
ALL OF THIS--
IT'S BECAUSE OF VICTORIA CARROWAY!

--ONE LAST TIME. YOU SURE YOU SAW HIM CLIMB IN THERE?
'CUZ WE CAN'T--
CAPTAIN!
O'MALLEY?? WHAT--WHAT THE HELL ARE YOU--
DAMN CHINK RIPPED MY FINGER OFF, BUT NO FUCKIN' WAY I'M SITTIN' THIS OUT.
Y'HEAR THAT?! THIS JOINT--
THIS "JOINT'S" PRACTICALLY A FOOTBALL FIELD, DETECTIVE. AND WITH THIS RAIN, HE COULD SNEAK PAST US WITH TWICE THE BACKUP.
SO LOSE THE HOOCH. WE'RE NOT DOING ANYTHING HALF-COCKED.
NO...
WE SURE AIN'T.

"WITHOUT THE OPERATION... WELL, MY FATHER'S DEATH CRUSHED MY MOTHER.
"AND AFTER A FEW YEARS...HER BODY WENT TOO.
"I BOUNCED BETWEEN ORPHANAGES UNTIL I WAS FINALLY OF AGE.
"BUT NO MATTER WHERE I WENT... CHINATOWN WAS HOME.
"LOS ANGELES'S ISN'T AS BIG AS SAN FRANCISCO'S, BUT EVERY DOLLAR I COULD SCRAPE, I MADE SURE I WAS LEARNING. ABOUT MY HERITAGE.
"EVERYTHING I'VE TRIED TO DO...WAS TO HELP FELLOW ORIENTALS.
"BUT... I HAVE A GWEILO'S FACE."

NO MATTER WHAT I DID.
MY FATHER TOLD MOTHER HE HAD A KID ON HIS WAY TO LOS ANGELES.
HE WAS JUST TOO AMBITIOUS TO SETTLE DOWN.
SO I PROMISED HER I'D FIND YOU, IVY-- ONE DAY--
AND, PROTECT YOU. LIKE A GOOD BROTHER.
YEAH...
THE ONLY THING MA EVER SAID ABOUT BA WAS HE THOUGHT HE WAS BETTER THAN US.
WELL, I JUST WANT TO HELP...
I'M SO GRATEFUL FOR HOLLY. IF I HADN'T MET HER, I'D STILL BE WANDERING TOWN...
I COULDN'T BELIEVE IT...
COMING ACROSS MY BEST FRIEND'S HALF BROTHER...?
YEAH...SO, UM, YOUR GRANDPARENTS ARE MILLIONAIRES? IF THEY'RE RICH, MAYBE--
OH, NOT ANYMORE.
THOSE GWEILO FUCKERS LOST IT ALL WHEN THE MARKET SANK.
BUT WE'VE GOT EACH OTHER NOW. WE'RE NOT ALONE ANYMORE.
TRUST ME, IT'S ALL FINALLY GOING TO BE OK.

VICTORIA?? WHAT ARE YOU TALKING ABOUT...?
YOU KNOW, NOT THAT LONG AGO, I WAS WHERE YOU ARE...
AND... WELL...
HEH.
YOU SHOULD FEEL IT...
HOW MUCH LYE BURNS.
HEY-- HOLD ON...
THEY LEFT ME FOR DEAD. DONNIE YAN, HIS PATHETIC BROTHER, VICTORIA CARROWAY--
DONNIE SHOT ME IN THE GODDAMN BACK! BUT I GOT AWAY BEFORE...
HEH. THEY MUST HAVE LOOKED SO HARD FOR ME...
BUT THEY DIDN'T KNOW ABOUT MY FACTORY. THE WOODWARD FACTORY...
BUT WHEN-- WHEN I GOT HERE...
HOLD ON, OK? WAIT!!!
IF I JUST ASKED WHAT YOU KNEW...
YOU'D LIE FOR THEM--THE CARROWAYS...
WOULDN'T YOU?

YOU DON'T **KNOW** WHAT IT'S LIKE.
AAAAAA!!

FOR YOUR FLESH AND BLOOD TO **HATE** YOU.
STOP--

YOU DON'T KNOW WHAT IT'S **LIKE**--TO KNOW THEY'RE **RIGHT**--
AAAAA!!

YOU HAVE NO IDEA--
--NO IDEA--

HEH.
HEHHEHHEH...

YOU...
YOU THINK **THAT'S** WHY THEY HATE...YOUR *GWEILO* FACE?

A FACE...WHO'S NEVER HAD TO WORRY ABOUT THE **COPS**...
ORIENTAL...WHEN **CONVENIENT**--

YOU THINK YOU'RE ONE OF **US?**

YOU'RE JUST A **HALF.** HALF **ORIENTAL.** HALF **MAN.** HALF--
LYE

SHUT UP!!

CAREFUL!! NOT... OVER THERE...
I...
...KNOCKED IT OVER...
...BURNED... SO MUCH...
THEY WERE CHEATERS, HOLLY. THEY SNUCK UP ON ME--
I KNOW, BUT IT'S OK...YOU CALLED, AND I'M HERE--
IT-- SPLASHED ON ME... THE LYE...
I...I GOT HERE AND WASN'T... CAREFUL.
SILAS-- LISTEN. I KNOW YOU WANTED TO HELP IVY BUT--
JUST FORGET HER--SHE'S ASHAMED OF US. LET'S TAKE THE MONEY AND--
NO!
IVY'S... FAMILY. FAMILY'S ALL WE HAVE...
YOU'LL SEE...WE'LL MAKE HER COME BACK...

YOU SEE?
HOW IT BURNS?
DO YOU? YOU SHOULD HAVE HAD A PLAN. LIKE ME. I THOUGHT EVERYTHING OUT...
KAK KAK
AND NOW-- NOW YOU'LL TELL ME EVERY--
?
DETECTIVE 347 POLICE
IS THIS...YOURS? WHY-- WHY WOULD YOU--?

UHHH!
BAM
!
DIE
HAKKK
HEAR ME--
LET-- LET GO
I SAID--
AK-- AK AK--
DIE--!

?
KRUNK
Shit shit shit--
Damn pipe--
busted--
Move quick--
Quick--
Woodward--
dropped his--
DO IT!

GO ON!
SHOOT! IT WON'T CHANGE ANYTHING!
Eyes...going...
End this-- fast or--
WHERE DID YOU GET THE BADGE FROM? HUH?
DO YOU WANT TO BE ONE OF THEM THAT BAD? THAT YOU'D PRETEND?
PRETEND TO BE A GWEILO? YOU'RE OKAY HURTING ORIENTALS IF THEY LET YOU PRE--
SHUT UP!

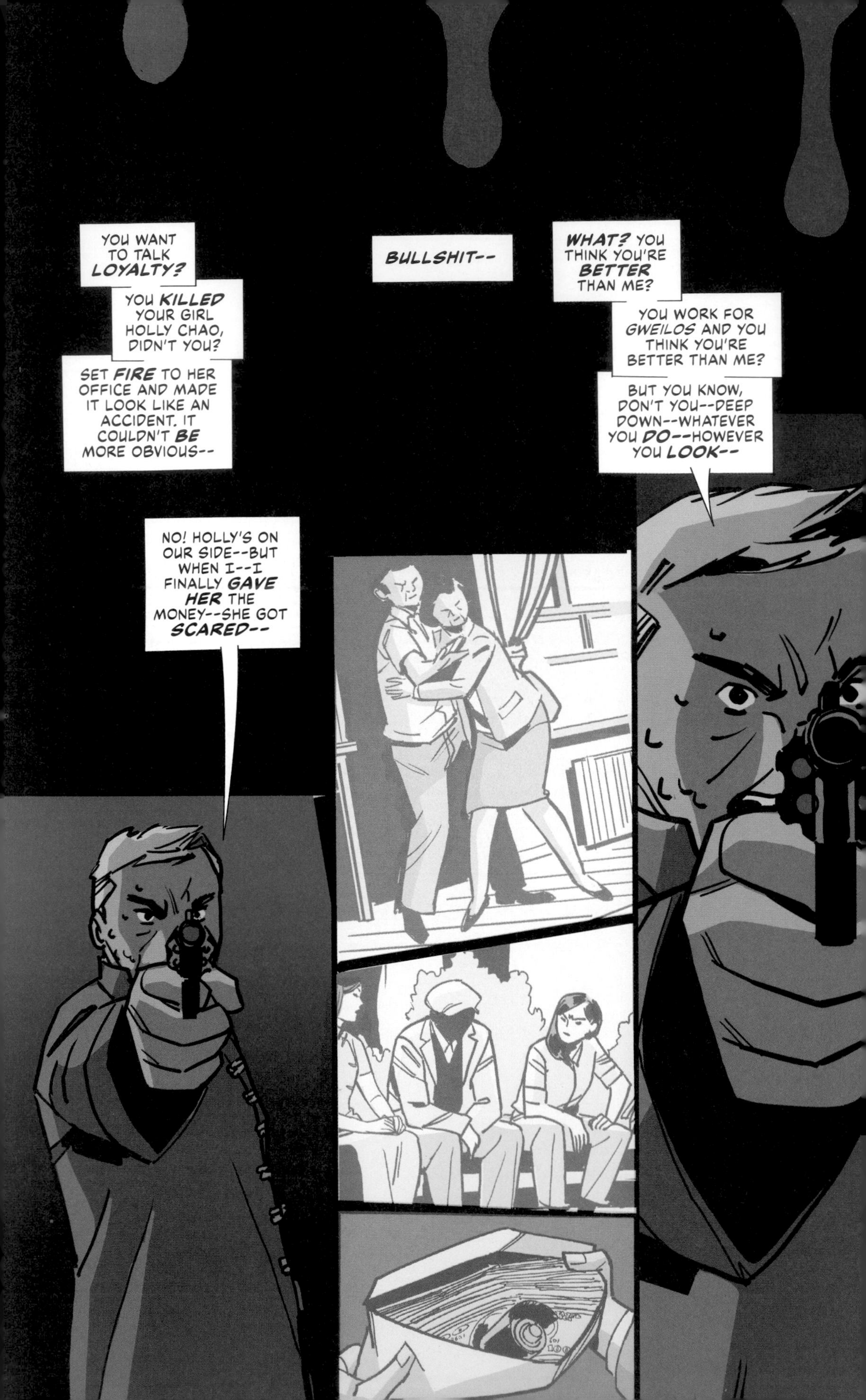
YOU WANT TO TALK LOYALTY?
YOU KILLED YOUR GIRL HOLLY CHAO, DIDN'T YOU?
SET FIRE TO HER OFFICE AND MADE IT LOOK LIKE AN ACCIDENT. IT COULDN'T BE MORE OBVIOUS--
BULLSHIT--
WHAT? YOU THINK YOU'RE BETTER THAN ME?
YOU WORK FOR GWEILOS AND YOU THINK YOU'RE BETTER THAN ME?
BUT YOU KNOW, DON'T YOU--DEEP DOWN--WHATEVER YOU DO--HOWEVER YOU LOOK--
NO! HOLLY'S ON OUR SIDE--BUT WHEN I--I FINALLY GAVE HER THE MONEY--SHE GOT SCARED--

To hell with Chinatown--
Frankie's killer **right here--**
THEY'LL ***NEVER*** SEE YOU--BECAUSE OF YOUR BLOOD--
Vision...going. Gun...heavy.
End this-- **fast--**
NOT IN THEIR ***WHITE*** WORLD.
AND NOT IN--

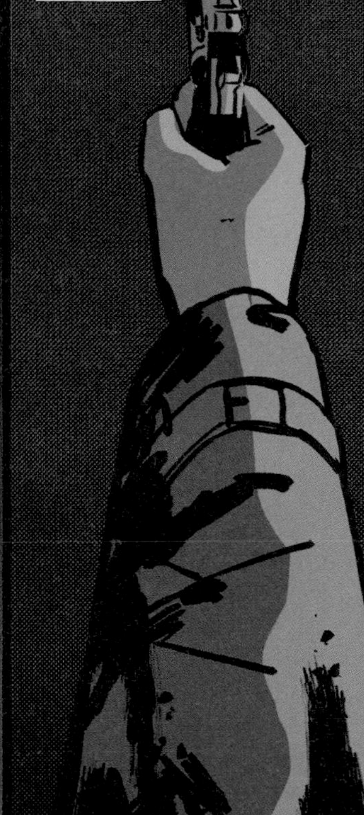

End this **now--**

BLAM
WHAT...?
Who the hell--?
But I know. Even though I've never seen him before... I know what he is.
Victoria's dog.

CHEATING... ALWAYS **CHEATING...**

KOFF *KOFF*

...THOUGHT EVERYTHING... OUT...

*She **played me.** And now the **bill's due--***

But not going down

without a

BAM

BAM

BAM

BLAM

THUD

BOOM

Go go go--
FREEZE!
Have to get out. **Has** to be a way--
FWOOOOSH
NO! DON'T LET HIM--
...THOUGHT EVERYTHING...
And I guess..."Hui Long" was right about one thing...

No.
STAY RIGHT WHERE YOU--
But...
BAM
BAM
It's only a matter of time.
Victoria... figured all the angles.
We are the same.
...EVERYTHING...

BOOM
BOOM

CHAPTER EIGHT

ART BY **DAVE JOHNSON**

ART BY **NIMIT MALAVIA**

They found shit
smeared on the doors
of two restaurants
down the street.

Some other people set the Jade Castle on fire, 'cuz they blamed Chinatown for Frankie Carroway's murder.
JADE CASTLE
I can't wait 'til I don't have to pass it EVERY walk home.
I can't wait 'til we don't have to be walked HOME every evening.
And I keep saying... Everything takes TIME.
Besides, closing the town EARLY to protect people was costing too much business.
tap tap
KEEP MOVING.
It's been TWO MONTHS since Americans stopped feeling safe in Chinatown.

A few in the neighborhood saw the Americans who did it, but they didn't bother to report it.
It's not like it'd do any good.
CHAPERONES made more sense. They walk all the women and seniors home. Armed with WHISTLES--
Hopefully enough to scare off attackers, but not enough to bother the COPS.
ALL RIGHT NOW...
Since the police increased patrols.
Since...

Ba wouldn't let me tell the police what happened.

No one else who was attacked that day talked either.
This was just the price you paid...
For starting over in America.

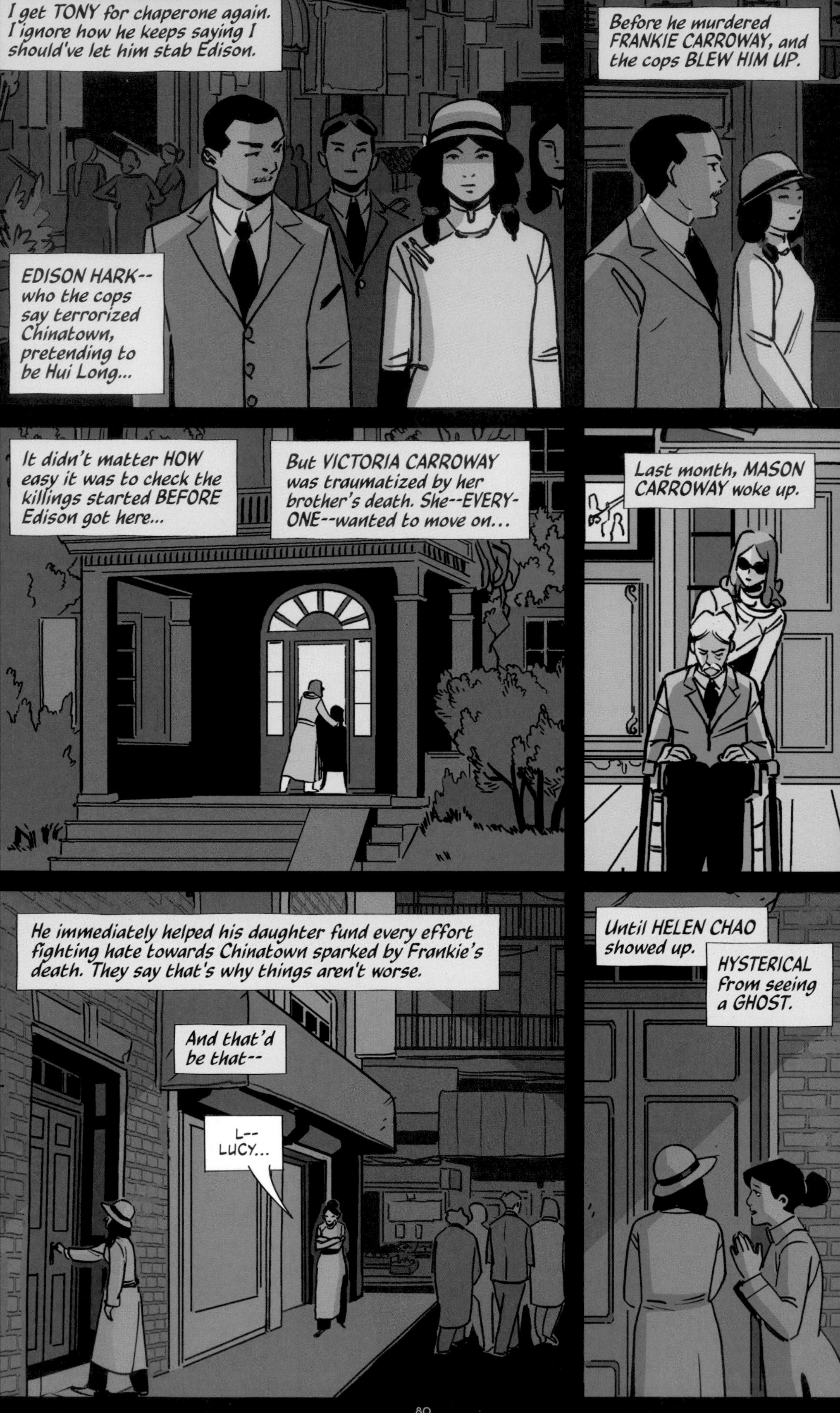
I get TONY for chaperone again. I ignore how he keeps saying I should've let him stab Edison.
EDISON HARK--who the cops say terrorized Chinatown, pretending to be Hui Long...
Before he murdered FRANKIE CARROWAY, and the cops BLEW HIM UP.
It didn't matter HOW easy it was to check the killings started BEFORE Edison got here...
But VICTORIA CARROWAY was traumatized by her brother's death. She--EVERY-ONE--wanted to move on...
Last month, MASON CARROWAY woke up.
He immediately helped his daughter fund every effort fighting hate towards Chinatown sparked by Frankie's death. They say that's why things aren't worse.
And that'd be that--
L--LUCY...
Until HELEN CHAO showed up.
HYSTERICAL from seeing a GHOST.

B-BA...?

He DOES this now.

He re-checks our locks every night. TWICE a night. At LEAST.

chik chak

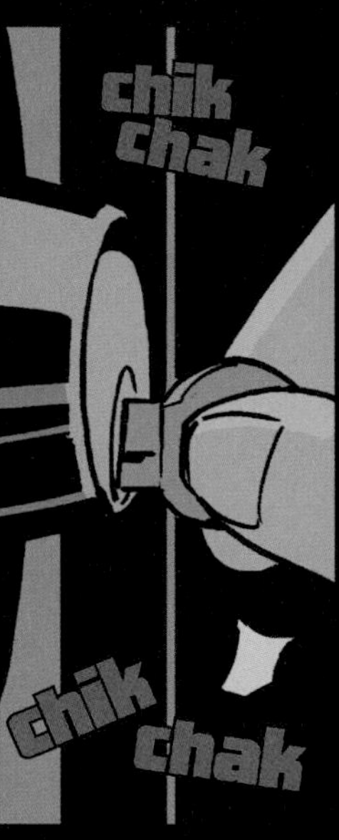

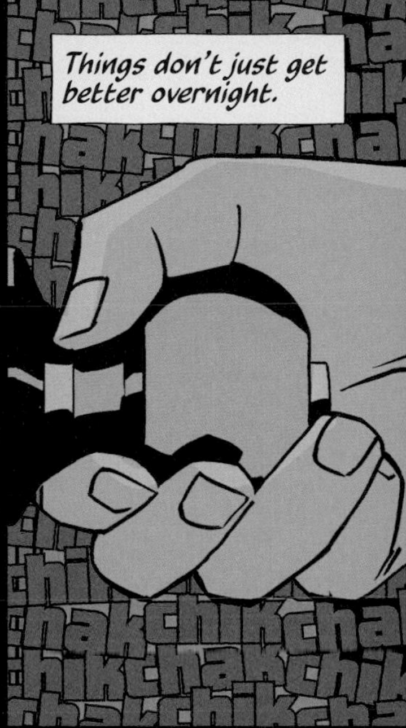

Helen's sister HOLLY was killed in a FIRE at work. It's a long story, but...I thought Hui Long set it, but since her body was BURNT beyond recognition...I ASKED AROUND.
Turns out, Holly'd spend smoke breaks walking through Portsmouth Square.
Every day at THREE. Which was...right BEFORE the fire.
So I KEPT asking. Because what if someone SAW her on that walk--what if she MISSED the fire and realized someone was out to GET her?
大廈
What if she went into hiding and was secretly OK ALL ALONG?
What if everything WASN'T horrible?
But...nobody saw her go on that walk.
Except a friend's grandfather. He saw her...a week LATER. On a TRAIN in the middle of the night.
And the only train leaving town THAT late was to SANTA CRUZ.

BOARDWALK
Helen didn't believe me when I told her. And then I DROPPED it all after Ba got hurt.
But now... Helen SWEARS she saw her sister outside their apartment. That Holly drove AWAY when Helen chased after her.
And I shouldn't waste TIME with cuckoo, but... well, I can catch the next train home in time to tuck Ba in...
Because what if I was right? What if everything wasn't horrible?
HEY! HAVEN'T SEEN YOU IN A WHILE! ANOTHER PISTACHIO SUNDAE?
I thought it'd be harder, getting people to recognize an old photo of Holly.
But this is the THIRD store now I've had to convince someone I'm NOT her.
That I'm just looking for a FRIEND.
Guess you stand out if you're ORIENTAL around here.

...DOESN'T SOUND LIKE SHE KNOWS WHAT SHE'S TALKING ABOUT... YOU'RE SAFE...
And THIS mister started looking suspicious the second he saw me...
UH...HI! I WAS WONDERING, IF YOU'VE SEEN--
BILL--YA KNUCKLEHEAD!! HOW'S TRICKS?
?
...
"...YOU'RE SAFE..."
Boys never notice their voices shift HIGHER when they're talking to girls.
ESPECIALLY when they're ATTRACTED to them.

HELLO, OPERATOR?
HI! I'VE A LITTLE BOY HERE WHO JUST GOT CUT OFF FROM HIS MOM--
OH MY GOD, **COULD** YOU RE-CONNECT US?
YEAH, AND IN CASE WE HAVE TO MOVE TO A NEW PHONE, I JUST WANT TO MAKE SURE I CAN READ THIS HANDWRITING...
I THINK IT'S A FIVE...? AND...A TWO? GOD, THIS LOOKS LIKE A Q...

!

HOLLY?
HOLLY CHAO?
NO...
OH NO...

NO, NO, IT'S OK. HE'S DEAD.
WOODWARD. IVY'S BROTHER.
YOU DON'T HAVE TO BE AFRAID OF HIM ANYMORE.

...TAKE OUT THEIR EYES??
YEAH, SOME NEIGHBOR TOLD IVY ABOUT THIS HATCHETMAN WHEN SHE WAS A KID, AND SHE'S BEEN OBSESSED EVER SINCE.

I'M SURPRISED SHE TOLD YOU. GOD, SILAS-- LATELY...SHE'S BEEN SO "HOLIER-THAN-THOU."
HOLLY...SHE'S JUST GOING THROUGH A LOT--

YEAH, IS THAT WHY SHE'S BLOWING US OFF?
SHE'LL BE HERE. THIS IS OUR SPOT. SHE WOULDN'T JUST LEAVE US...

"I MEAN, IVY KNOWS SHE'S MADE MISTAKES. BUT SHE'S DOING EVERYTHING SHE CAN TO CHANGE. TO BE BETTER.
"SHE JUST NEEDS HELP. AND TIME. THE SAME WAY SHE'S HELPED ME START OVER, FIND A JOB--"
"GOD, HOW DOES SHE DO IT? EVERYONE IVY MEETS FEEL SORRY FOR HER. THEY WANT TO PROTECT HER.
"SHE'S THE SMARTEST PERSON I'VE EVER MET, AND YOU KNOW THE ONLY THING SHE WANTS?
"TO GET AWAY FROM ANYTHING-- ME, YOU, ANYTHING--THAT REMINDS HER OF WHO SHE IS OR WHERE SHE'S FROM."

THAT BITCH LIVES ON A MILLIONAIRE'S ESTATE AND HAS SHE EVER INVITED US--
HEY!
DON'T YOU EVER FUCKING TALK ABOUT MY SISTER LIKE THAT.
...
IT'S JUST...YOU DON'T KNOW HER LIKE I DO.
I SAW IT THE SECOND I INTRODUCED YOU TWO. THE WAY SHE SQUIRMED. YOU WERE SUDDENLY IN HER LIFE--I WAS BACK--
RIGHT WHEN SHE FINALLY GOT HER HOOKS IN THE OLD MAN...
THE OLD...? MASON CARROWAY? HE'S OLD ENOUGH TO--
YOU'RE NOT LISTENING--IVY'D DO ANYTHING IF IT GOT HER OUT OF CHINATOWN.
BUT IT DOESN'T MATTER.
VICTORIA CARROWAY ALMOST FIRED HER WHEN SHE LEARNED HER OLD MAN HAD FEELINGS FOR IVY.
WHAT?
YEAH, IVY HAD TO BEG...
"IT INCENSED SILAS. VICTORIA REJECTING IVY? ESPECIALLY CONSIDERING..."

IVY'D **OVERHEARD** VICTORIA ADMITTING TO FRIENDS SHE HAD...**BEEN** WITH AN ORIENTAL ONCE.
SILAS STARTED **BLACKMAILING** HER BECAUSE HE COULDN'T STAND THE HYPOCRISY...
HE WAS SO **PROUD** WHEN HE TOLD IVY SHE COULD QUIT HER JOB.

THAT **NOTHING** WAS STANDING BETWEEN HER AND MASON ANYMORE...
BUT...
GOD...HOW DO YOU EVEN **KNOW** ABOUT SILAS?

SILAS. IS THAT HIS FULL NAME? **SILAS WOODWARD?**
YEAH.
WELL, IT'S...A **STORY.** THE IMPORTANT THING IS YOU'RE **SAFE** NOW. I DON'T KNOW HOW YOU COULD STAND **HIDING** FOR SO LONG.

YEAH, LIVING ALONE LIKE THIS WAS DRIVING ME CRAZY.
I WISH **I** COULD. BUT I'D NEVER BE ABLE TO AFFORD...
Actually, YEAH...

I could NEVER afford a place like this, and Holly's at LEAST as broke as me. I assumed she was staying with friends, so how--?
OH NO

I KNEW IT WAS DUMB GOING HOME.

"COME ON. YOU MIGHT AS WELL HELP ME MOVE..."

SO...THAT GUY CALLING YOU--IS HE YOUR NEW SQUEEZE OR SOMETHING?

PLEASE. HE'S SOME SAP TO RUN ERRANDS. ORIENTALS AROUND HERE ATTRACT TOO MUCH ATTENTION.
LOOK, EVEN IF YOU DON'T CARE ABOUT ANYONE ELSE. YOUR FAMILY THINKS YOU'RE DEAD.

"THEY'LL BE FINE. SOONER OR LATER, I KNEW HELEN'D FIND THE CASH I HID.
"BUT I WAS AT MAHJONG PARLORS, GOSSIPING THAT HUI LONG WAS BACK..."

...MAKING SURE THERE WAS AN EASY TRAIL TO FOLLOW.
SO YOU FIGURED, YOU'D COVER YOUR TRACKS BY SETTING A FIRE THAT KILLED YOUR CO-WORKERS.
SILAS TOOK CARE OF THE FIRE. I DIDN'T KNOW--

OH, CUT THE ***BULL***--YOU NEEDED PEOPLE TO FIND SOMEONE ***ELSE'S*** BODY IN THAT FIRE!
NO!
YOU ***KNEW*** WOODWARD WAS A PSYCHOPATH!

...NO.
HE WASN'T ALWAYS CRAZY. NOT...NOT AT FIRST...

HE JUST...HE WAS SO ***PROUD*** OF HIS ORIENTAL FAMILY. EVEN THOUGH NO ONE SAW ***HIM*** AS ORIENTAL.
EVEN WHEN HE WASN'T... ***REASONABLE*** ANYMORE, I WANTED TO ***BELIEVE*** HIM.
HE WAS SO ***SMART.*** HE GOT THIS PLACE--MONEY TO TIDE ME OVER...

WHEN HE WAS ***DONE*** GETTING EVEN, HE'D COME BACK WITH ***HIS*** SHARE, BUT...
BUT NOW HE'S ***DEAD.***

IF YOU WANTED TO GET AWAY SO BAD, WHY EVEN COME BACK?

WHY GIVE HELEN THE ***CHANCE*** TO SEE YOU--?

HEY, ***HEY***--WHERE DO YOU THINK ***YOU'RE*** GOING?

YOU THINK I DON'T NOTICE HOW YOU KEEP DRIFTING BACK THERE--!
AAAH!!
HFFF!
UHH!
Get the gun get the gun get the
NO!!

UHHH!!!
WHAT THE HELL?
I COULD HAVE SHOT YOU...!
WHY... WHY ARE YOU DOING THIS? FOR MONEY? THAT'S IT?
THAT'S IT--?
YOU WANT TO KNOW WHY I WENT BACK? HUH?
BECAUSE I READ IN THE PAPERS FRANKIE CARROWAY DIED. IN CHINATOWN. AND WHEN SILAS NEVER SHOWED...
I NEEDED TO KNOW MY FAMILY WAS OK. 'CUZ I KNEW IF THEY WEREN'T?
I'D NEVER HEAR.
'CUZ THEY DON'T SEE US. NOT THE AMERICANS. NOT THEIR PAPERS...
IVY GOT THAT. YOU WANT TO KNOW WHERE "HUI LONG" CAME FROM?
SHE KNEW AS LONG AS EVERYONE WAS SCARED, THEY WOULDN'T PAY ATTENTION TO ANYTHING ELSE.
BECAUSE THAT'S WHAT HOLDS CHINATOWN TOGETHER.
FEAR.

'CUZ NO MATTER HOW MUCH THINGS SEEM TO GET BETTER, WE KNOW--
IT CAN GO AWAY. JUST LIKE THAT. WHEN NO ONE'S LOOKING. BECAUSE NOBODY CARES--
AND THEY NEVER WILL.
NO...
EVERYTHING JUST...
TAKES TIME...
AND HOW MANY PEOPLE WILL BE HURT WHILE YOU KEEP WAITING?
I--
...I DON'T KNOW.
I--I JUST...
I'M SORRY.
I REALLY AM...

SLAM

VROOOOOOOOOMMM

I tell myself Holly walked away because she's not a KILLER.
But she SAID it--she felt sorry for me.

Even though my cab's long gone, it was easy to call another to pick me up. Despite everything, I'm home to tuck Ba in.
chikchakchikchak

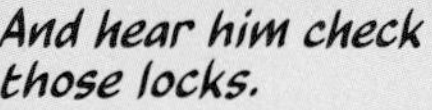
And hear him check those locks.

And I've no more lies to tell myself. About things taking time. All I've left from the pit of my stomach...

Is FIRE.
'Cuz at the end of the day, FIRE'S more important than brains.

And I don't care that I promised myself LAST WEEK I'd never come back here, I'm here NOW--

Talking to Edison Hark.
OK...
WHAT DO YOU WANT ME TO DO?

CHAPTER NINE

ART BY **DAVE JOHNSON**

ART BY **OLIVIER TADUC**

GET BACK!! THIS WHOLE PLACE'LL BLOW AT ANY SECOND!
...THOUGHT...
...EVERYTHING... OUT...

NO! IF HE GETS AWAY--
THEY...

GET BACK! GET BACK--!!
THEY CAN'T...

Silas Woodward really had planned for everything.
...WIN...

BOOM
Well... Almost.

Even he couldn't predict the storm hammering the city...
Would flood the sewer tunnel he was planning to escape through.
"YOU'LL SEE, SON. SOMEDAY, WE'LL BE HOME, AND EVERYTHING WILL BE BETTER."

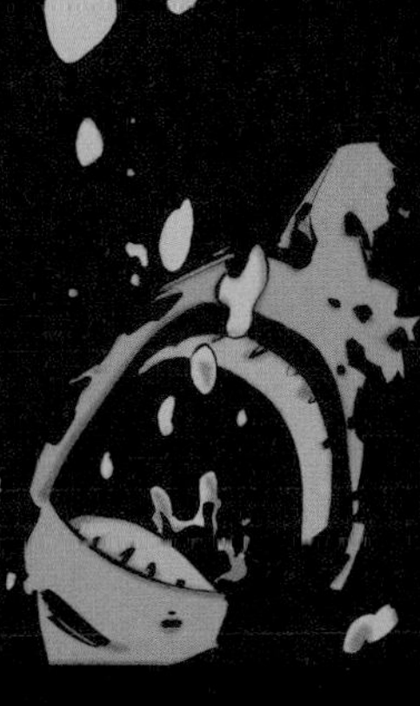

SOMEDAY...? BUT YOU TOLD MA WE'D GO STRAIGHT HOME...
AIYA, NOT THAT STUPID HUT. I MEAN, HOME. GUANGZHOU. CHINA.
DON'T BE DUMB LIKE ME AND YOUR MA. THINKING JUST BECAUSE THERE'S WORK SOMEWHERE...
Pfft. YOU WANT TO BE LIKE YOUR FATHER? TO ONLY KNOW HOW TO RUN AWAY?
MAMA, FRANKIE'LL STILL BE MY FRIEND EVEN IF I DON'T PLAY WITH HIM FOR ONE--
YOU HAVE A CHANCE ANY CHINESE BOY WOULD KILL FOR. I DIDN'T RAISE YOU TO BE STUPID.
IT'S FINE, SIR. I WASN'T SUSPENDED--
WHY WOULD THEY SUSPEND YOU? THOSE BOYS ATTACKED YOU! SAYING YOU DON'T BELONG?!
IT'S OK--
NO, IT'S--!

YOU'RE JUST CHINESE. DON'T FORGET THAT. BECAUSE THEY WON'T.
IN THIS COUNTRY, CHINESE IS ALL YOU GET TO BE.
YOU CAN BE MORE THAN YOUR FATHER. OR ME.
PEOPLE HERE LIKE YOU.
DON'T EVER GIVE THEM A REASON TO REGRET IT.
...
EDISON, YOU'RE ONE OF US. A CARROWAY.
NO MATTER WHAT, NO ONE CAN SAY YOU DON'T BELONG HERE, DO YOU UNDERSTAND?

...

...OF COURSE, SIR.

KAK KAK KAK
I came to **miles** from Woodward's paint factory. The current spitting me **clear** cross town.

Yeah, Woodward **had** thought of everything...

Including arrangements with a **black market doctor** ready to give him a new **face** so he could **disappear.**

One not choosy **where** his cash came from, and too scared of "Tong retribution" to touch a **cent** more than promised.

He even had a **flophouse** to keep on-the-lam bruisers needing more recovery.
YOU KNOW, YOU ***ALWAYS*** HAVE ME BRING FONG FONG...

BUT YOU NEVER EAT IT WHILE IT'S HOT.
I paid the doc to contact Lucy.
FONG FONG
She was too sharp to buy me being Hui Long and too decent to settle for less than the truth.
Besides, I needed her if Victoria was going to pay.
It's been four months since the explosion.
Lucy and I've been at it for weeks.
Since she changed her mind after my first offer, deciding to come back and do my legwork after all.
In our time apart, she found a friend of Ivy's--Holly Chao--a girl everyone thought dead... a girl with answers.
SO-- COMBINING WHAT HOLLY TOLD ME AND... EVERYTHING ELSE--

"WE KNOW SILAS WOODWARD THOUGHT VICTORIA WAS STANDING IN THE WAY OF IVY BEING WITH HER FATHER, MASON CARROWAY.
"AND THE IDEA ANYONE IN HIS FAMILY WASN'T GOOD ENOUGH INFURIATED WOODWARD, SO HE STARTED FOLLOWING VICTORIA.
"HE WAS HOPING TO FIND SOMETHING TO MAKE HER BACK OFF. IT WAS AROUND THEN VICTORIA WAS HAVING NON-STOP MEETINGS WITH TERENCE CHANG TO TALK ABOUT MASON'S INVESTMENTS IN CHINATOWN."
BUT THE MORE WOODWARD WATCHED THEM, THE MORE HE THOUGHT, THEY WERE, UM, YOU KNOW...
HE THOUGHT THEY WERE BUMPING UGLIES.
'CEPT THERE WAS NO PROOF. SO HE STARTED FOLLOWING TERENCE. MAYBE HE'D SLIP UP.
"AND HE DID. WOODWARD SHADOWED HIM, SNAPPING SHOTS OF HIM DOING THE DEED...WITH A FELLA.
"AND THAT'S WHEN--FOR ALL HIS TALK OF ORIENTAL CAMARADERIE--
"WOODWARD SET OUT TO GET THE CHINATOWN MONEY AND RESPECT HE FIGURED HE DESERVED.
"'CUZ TERENCE'S BEST FRIENDS-- BENNIE AND DONNIE YAN... WERE TWO OF CHINATOWN'S RICHEST AND MOST INFLUENTIAL BIRDS.
"WHO WERE DEAD SET ON PROTECTING SOMEONE AS IMPORTANT TO CHINATOWN..."

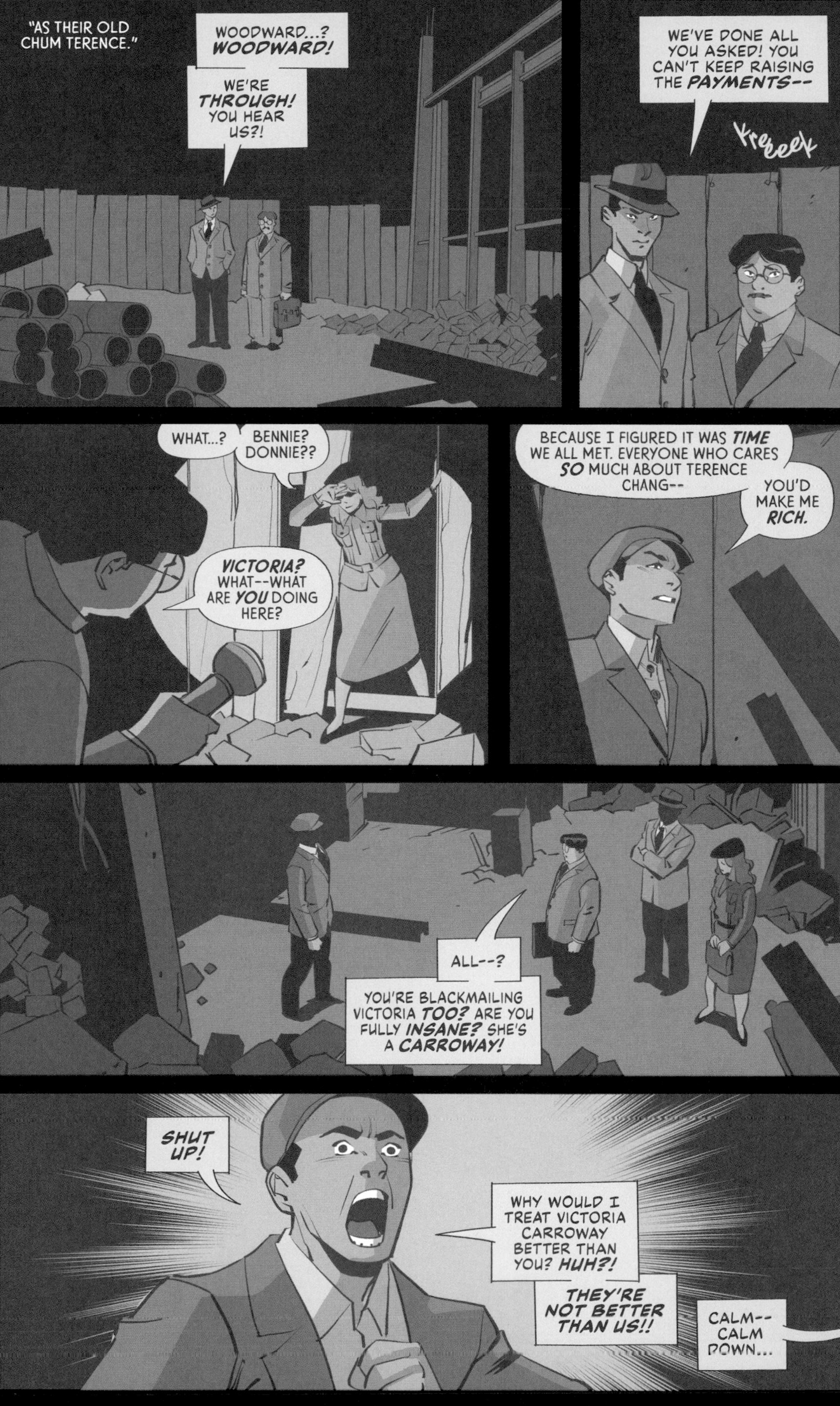
"AS THEIR OLD CHUM TERENCE."
WOODWARD...? WOODWARD!
WE'RE THROUGH! YOU HEAR US?!
WE'VE DONE ALL YOU ASKED! YOU CAN'T KEEP RAISING THE PAYMENTS--
kreeeek
WHAT...?
BENNIE? DONNIE??
VICTORIA? WHAT--WHAT ARE YOU DOING HERE?
BECAUSE I FIGURED IT WAS TIME WE ALL MET. EVERYONE WHO CARES SO MUCH ABOUT TERENCE CHANG--
YOU'D MAKE ME RICH.
ALL--?
YOU'RE BLACKMAILING VICTORIA TOO? ARE YOU FULLY INSANE? SHE'S A CARROWAY!
SHUT UP!
WHY WOULD I TREAT VICTORIA CARROWAY BETTER THAN YOU? HUH?!
THEY'RE NOT BETTER THAN US!!
CALM-- CALM DOWN...

LOOK! WE BROUGHT ALL THE CASH, OK? DONNIE... SHOW HIM!
UH...YEAH. YEAH. WE BROUGHT...
EVERYTHING.
BLAM
AHH!!
YOU IDIOT--! HE HAS SOMEONE WHO'LL RELEASE TERENCE'S PHOTOS AT THE FIRST SIGN--
IT DOESN'T MATTER...WE PLANNED FOR THIS TOO--
WAIT...WHY DO YOU CARE WHAT HAPPENS TO TERENCE?
I DON'T... I MEAN--
SHUT UP! BOTH OF YOU!!
WOODWARD--
HE'S GONE...
"AFTER THAT, WOODWARD LAID LOW, LICKING HIS WOUNDS..."

ACCORDING TO YOU, HE REMEMBERED THE HUI LONG LEGEND IVY TOLD HIM ABOUT. USED IT AS A SMOKESCREEN--
FIGURING IF HE WENT AFTER THE THREE DIRECTLY-- ONCE ONE CROAKED-- THE OTHERS'D KNOW IT WAS HIM--
TAKING IT OUT ON IVY.
BUT STILL-- WHY WAS VICTORIA THERE IN THE FIRST PLACE?
HOLLY SAID WOODWARD WAS BLACKMAILING HER TOO.
THAT THERE WAS SO MUCH CARROWAY MONEY IN CHINATOWN THEY COULDN'T AFFORD TERENCE'S SECRET COMING OUT.
BULL.
THE CARROWAYS COULD LOSE THREE TIMES THAT AND STILL BARELY NOTICE.
WHICH MEANS, VICTORIA LET HIM THINK THAT...
'CUZ IT WAS SAFER THAN THE TRUTH.
AHHH!!
EDISON!

IT'S...ALL RIGHT...
JUST NEED...
REST. YOU'RE PUSHING YOURSELF TOO HARD.
SHE CAN'T... GET AWAY WITH...
SHE WON'T. I'VE BEEN KEEPING AN EYE ON TERENCE LIKE YOU SAID, AND...I DON'T KNOW WHY, BUT HE'S SO CARELESS...
"JUST...GET SOME REST, AND WE'LL GET BACK AT IT TOMORROW...
"WE'LL GET THEM."
CREEEEKKK

HEH. I KNEW IF I COULD ESCAPE THAT HELL-PIT...
YOU WOULDN'T DISAPPOINT.
PFFFT
PFFFT
PFFFT
PFFFT
RIGHT?

!
He had no idea how long I'd been waiting for him.
Months thinking about his mug.
And the nagging feeling...
I'd seen it before.
FONG FONG
Which meant if he was looking for me, he might shadow the girl.
So I made things easy for him...
FONG FONG
As easy as planning a lame duck charade-- even to Lucy to sell the act.
And, of course, noticing a new car parked on this otherwise lonely street.

AHH!!
BLAM

YOU GOT ME, OK? JUST... ⇒AH⇐ GET THAT OUT OF MY FACE...

I'LL--I'LL TELL YOU WHAT YOU WANT TO KNOW.

THAT'S...WHY YOU *LURED* ME HERE, RIGHT?

RIGHT?
TALK--
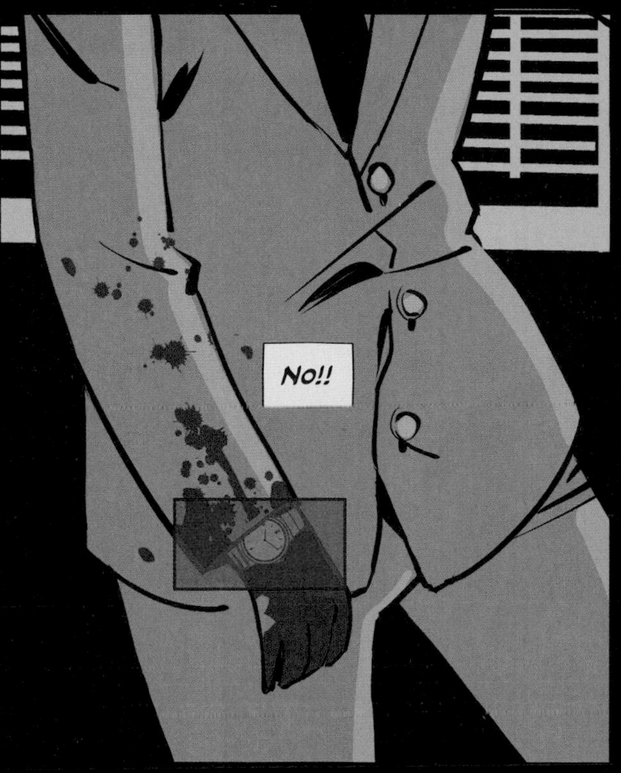
No!!
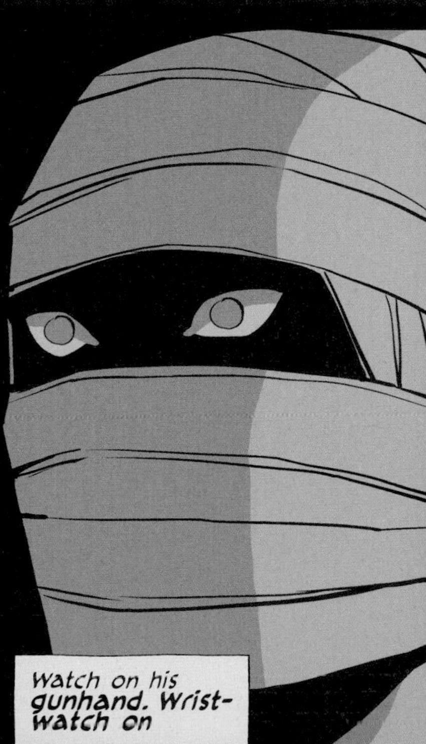
Watch on his gunhand. Wrist-watch on

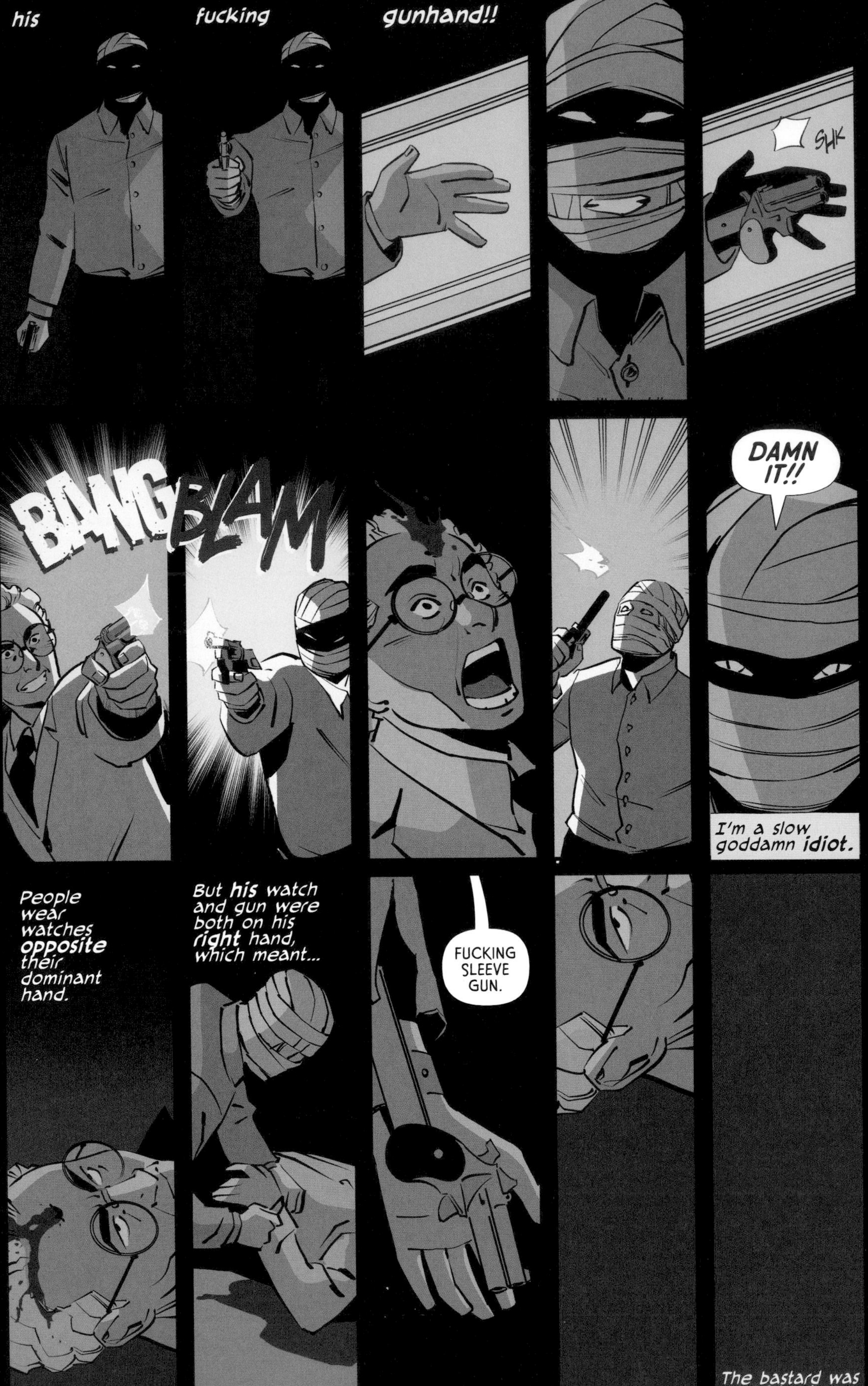
his
fucking
gunhand!!
SHK
BANG
BLAM
DAMN IT!!
I'm a slow goddamn idiot.
People wear watches opposite their dominant hand.
But his watch and gun were both on his right hand, which meant...
FUCKING SLEEVE GUN.
The bastard was ambidextrous.

And while Lucy was annoyed I'd lied to her, she reminded me we had other plays. 'Cuz Terence had been sloppy.
Twice this week he'd gone to this apartment on the outskirts of Chinatown--the home of a friend of Victoria's.
I DON'T GET IT...
YOU SAID THE DOCTOR GAVE YOU A NEW FACE, SO WHY HAVEN'T YOU TAKEN YOUR BANDAGES OFF?
AREN'T YOU CURIOUS WHAT IT LOOKS LIKE?
IT'D STILL BE ORIENTAL. AND IT'S EASIER BEING A CHINAMAN ON THE LAM IF NO ONE KNOWS YOU'RE ONE.
...
HOW'S YOUR BA?
...OK. STILL... CHECKING HIS LOCKS.
SO, HOW'RE YOU?
I JUST... KEEPING THINKING ABOUT WHAT HOLLY SAID.
THAT NO MATTER WHAT--
NOBODY CARES...AND NOBODY EVER WILL.

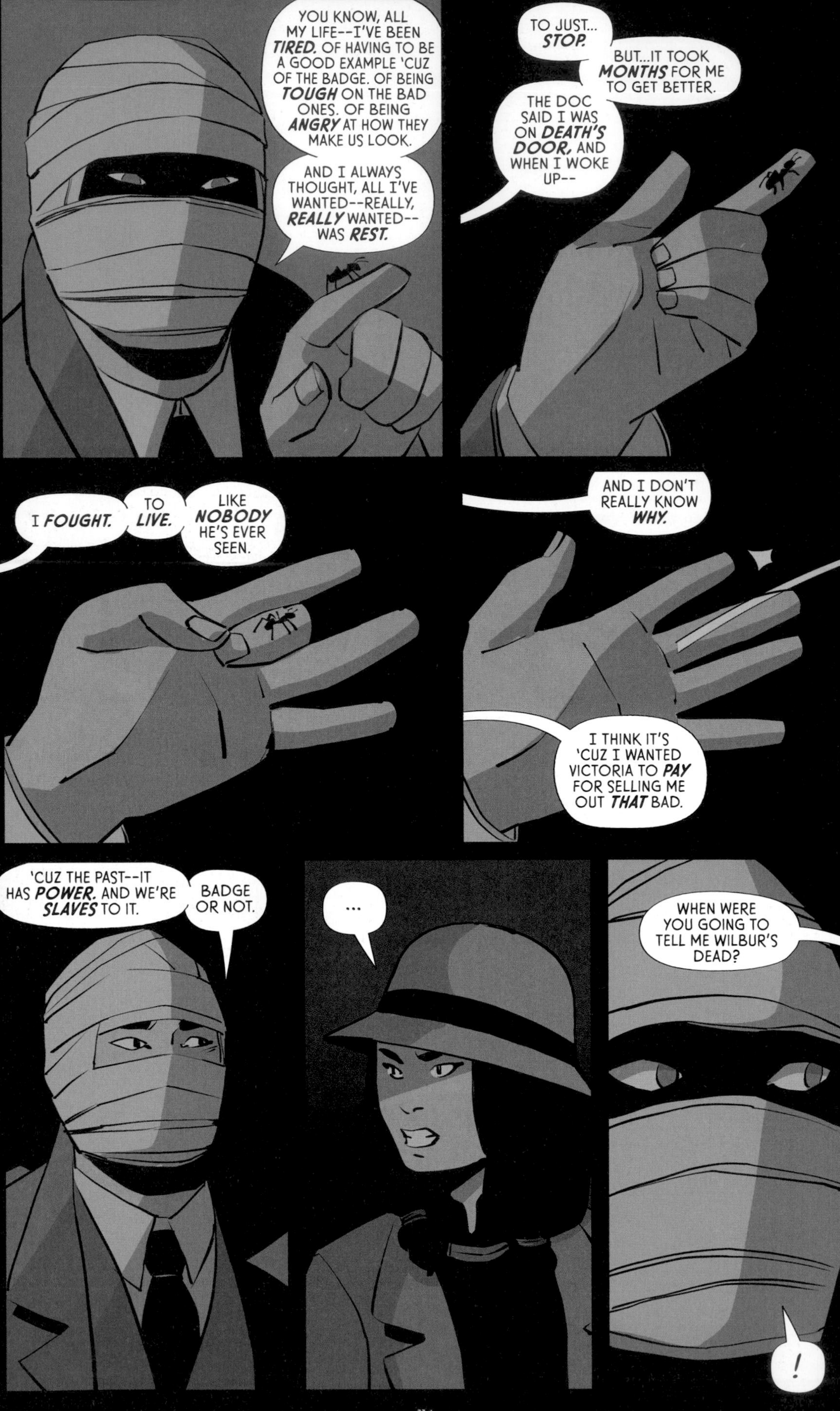
YOU KNOW, ALL MY LIFE--I'VE BEEN TIRED. OF HAVING TO BE A GOOD EXAMPLE 'CUZ OF THE BADGE. OF BEING TOUGH ON THE BAD ONES. OF BEING ANGRY AT HOW THEY MAKE US LOOK.
AND I ALWAYS THOUGHT, ALL I'VE WANTED--REALLY, REALLY WANTED--WAS REST.
TO JUST... STOP.
BUT...IT TOOK MONTHS FOR ME TO GET BETTER.
THE DOC SAID I WAS ON DEATH'S DOOR, AND WHEN I WOKE UP--
I FOUGHT.
TO LIVE.
LIKE NOBODY HE'S EVER SEEN.
AND I DON'T REALLY KNOW WHY.
I THINK IT'S 'CUZ I WANTED VICTORIA TO PAY FOR SELLING ME OUT THAT BAD.
'CUZ THE PAST--IT HAS POWER. AND WE'RE SLAVES TO IT.
BADGE OR NOT.
...
WHEN WERE YOU GOING TO TELL ME WILBUR'S DEAD?
!

I FOUND OUT BEFORE I EVEN WENT TO SEE YOU, YOU KNOW. I WROTE HIS SISTER.
SHE TOLD ME EVERYTHING. HOW YOU HAD TO ARREST HIM. HOW HE WAS MURDERED IN JAIL. THE WHOLE NINE.
AND I'VE BEEN WAITING FOR YOU TO SAY, HEY, I DON'T KNOW WHAT I COULD HAVE DONE, BUT I'M SORRY.
BUT YOU DIDN'T, 'CUZ YOU WERE SCARED I WOULDN'T HELP, RIGHT?
BUT... HERE I AM ANYWAY.
BECAUSE YOU AND HOLLY ARE FULL OF IT.
YOU DON'T HAVE YOUR BADGE ANYMORE. YOU'VE GOT A NEW FACE-- A CLEAN SLATE, AND ALL YOU CAN SAY IS YOU'RE A SLAVE.
AND MAYBE THAT'S TRUE--
OR MAYBE THAT'S JUST EASIER THAN ADMITTING YOU'RE THAT ASHAMED OF WHAT YOU ARE.
BULL--
YOU SAID IT. YOU DON'T WANT THOSE BANDAGES OFF, 'CUZ AS LONG AS THEY'RE ON--
NO ONE KNOWS YOU'RE ORIENTAL.

HOLD--
HOLD ON...
WAIT--

IT'S
TIME.

And with that...
THAT HAS TO BE HIM, RIGHT?

Showtime.

Lucy got word out to them both that the other wanted to meet "at the usual spot." And...

It was that easy.

Almost insultingly. They'd been careful for so long. Why be sloppy now?

Still, it was opportunity. Just pictures of them in a room together at this time of night?

It'd ruin them both. Giving me leverage to pry out real answers.

NOK NOK
Even if I promised Lucy we were bluffing.
And maybe I was. And maybe I wasn't.
Because Victoria... After selling me out, she had to--
Pay...
TERENCE-- OH GOD, OH GOD...!
I CAN'T... I CAN'T ANYMORE...
PLEASE...
IT'S BEEN MONTHS. YOU CAN'T KEEP CALLING ME LIKE THIS...
?

I CAN'T HELP YOU IF YOU DON'T TELL ME WHAT'S WRONG...
PLEASE... JUST PLEASE...

WHAT THE HELL DID YOU GET YOURSELF INTO, VICTORIA?
"I MEAN, WHAT THE HECK?"

YOU SAID WE'D CONFRONT THEM!! NOW THEY KNOW SOMEONE TRICKED THEM INTO MEETING EACH OTHER.
WE CAN GET THEM WHENEVER WE WANT. THEY'RE CLEARLY NOT LOOKING OUT FOR THEMSELVES ANYMORE.

...THE BANK MANAGER SAID FATHER VISITED AFTER IVY'S DISAPPEARANCE, ALMOST AS IF...
HE WAS QUIETLY PAYING A RANSOM.

NO, I WANT TO KNOW EVERYTHING WHEN I CONFRONT VICTORIA.
WHAT ELSE IS THERE TO KNOW?

...THOUSANDS UNACCOUNTED FOR. HE WITHDREW THEM EVERY THIRD OF THE MONTH--GOING BACK MONTHS.

SNPP

IN A FEW DAYS, IT'LL BE THE *THIRD* OF THE MONTH.
AND LAST WE TALKED, VICTORIA WAS CONCERNED ABOUT MASON'S *REGULAR WITHDRAWALS* FROM THE FAMILY SAFETY DEPOSIT BOX *EVERY* THIRD OF THE MONTH.

SNPP

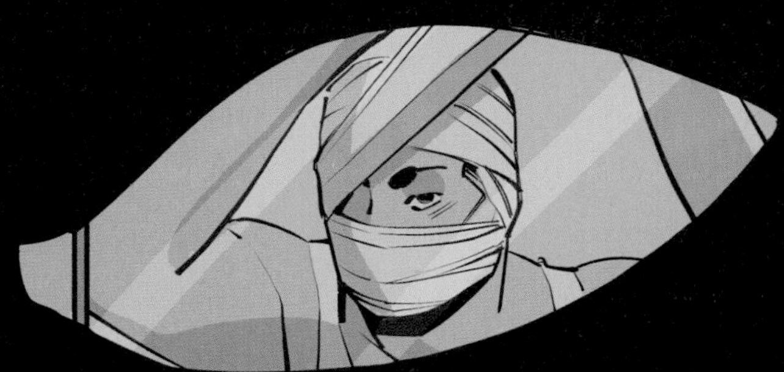
SHE WAS WORRIED HE WAS BEING *BLACKMAILED.*
NOW, SHE *COULD* HAVE SAID ALL THAT TO THROW ME OFF, BUT THEN WHY PULL OUT *ACTUAL* BOOKS TO SHOW ME?

UNLESS... SHE REALLY *WANTED* MY HELP, BECAUSE IT WAS LEGITIMATELY *VEXING* HER.
MAYBE SHE HADN'T DECIDED TO SELL ME OUT AT THAT POINT.

SO *WHAT?* WE'RE GOING TO STOP EVERYTHING JUST ON *THAT?*
AND...WHY EVERY *THIRD* OF THE MONTH? WHAT'S SO IMPORTANT ABOUT THE *THIRD?*
PLENTY, I'M SURE. BUT FOR *ME,* ON THE THIRD OF THE MONTH A LONG TIME AGO, A MAN NAMED *MICHAEL MARTINEZ...*

HE MURDERED MY MOTHER.

CHAPTER TEN

EDISON HARK
IN
THE GOOD ASIAN

DIRECTED BY
PICHETSHOTE
and TEFENKGI
LOUGHRIDGE • POWELL

With
LUCY FAN

ART BY DAVE JOHNSON

ART BY **ALEXANDRE TEFENKGI**

4 DAYS AGO
...WHEN I BROUGHT YOUR-- -A-HURM--HOUSEWARMING CAKE, YOU MENTIONED YOU'D NEVER SEEN A THIN MAN PICTURE--AND I...HAPPEN TO HAVE AN EXTRA--
YOU DO??
I MEAN...UH, IF YOU'RE ASKIN', I'D LOVE TA GO, WINSTON...
IF YER ASKIN'.
UH, YES. YES, I AM, ACTUALLY.
I'D HAVE VISITED SOONER, BUT YOUR, UM, FRIEND WAS OVER...
UH, YEAH...THAT'S JUST--MY, UH...OLDER BROTHER.
HE'S LOTS OLDER.
OH!! WONDERFUL--!
I MEAN...IT'S WONDERFUL YOU HAVE A BROTHER THAT VISITS SO--
?
!
RUBY...? WHAT'S WRONG?
UH...
NOTHIN', I JUST...
NOTHIN'.

NNNNHHH!
I...I DON'T KNOW WHO YOU THINK YOU ARE, SHOWING UP--
SHOWING UP IN OUR HOME IN THE MIDDLE...
WAS A TIME YOU'D ASK BEFORE WALLOPING A FELLA.
BUT I'M GUESSING THAT'S THE CONSCIENCE GNAWING, HUH?
IS THAT WHY YOU'RE GETTING OUT OF--?
HHNN!!
BUT YOU'RE A LONG WAY FROM YOUR BEST RIGHT NOW, AIN'T YOU?
IF YOU WERE AS FAMILIAR WITH ME AS YOU PRETEND, YOU'D KNOW I CAN PUT YOU DOWN REGARDLESS--
OF COURSE YOU CAN.
'CUZ NO MATTER WHAT YOU'VE DONE, THERE'S NO WAY I'D HIT BACK.
COME ON, VICTORIA...
YOU KNOW WHO I AM.

HHH!!
LISTEN, YOU. IF I HAD A NICKEL FOR EVERY MAN WHO'S UNDER-ESTIMATED ME--
YOU'RE A MILLIONAIRE. YOU DO.
...
ED-- EDISON?
I'M SORRY, I'M SO SO SORRY... I--I WAS JUST TRYING TO...
IT'S OK, IT'S OK.
...JUST TELL ME EVERYTHING.

3 DAYS AGO
SAL'S
(2)
still can't tell you where
I'm at, but promis I'm all rite.
I shouldn't even say that
much, but my hole life you're
the only person ever
looked out for me + always
had my back.
Promice I'll rite back soon.
-Ethel
KREEK
WHAT...?
IS--IS SOMEONE THERE...?

And Victoria confirms it **all.**

From being blackmailed by **Silas Woodward--**"an American claiming to be Ivy's brother"--who started blackmailing Victoria and others to help his sister--unbeknownst to Ivy.

But while it started small--money or else he'd out Terence Chang...things **escalated.**

Woodward **enjoyed** his newfound power over Victoria as well as **Bennie** and **Donnie Yan.** All three wishing to protect Terence **without him ever knowing.**

After Bennie failed to **kill** Woodward, the three knew he'd return for **payback.**

Weeks passed. The anxiety **eating** away at Victoria...

Until she overheard Mason and Ivy **arguing.**

When pressed, Ivy revealed she had a **brother** who'd **gone missing.** She was upset Mason wouldn't help look for him.

And Victoria saw an **opportunity--** to **stop** Silas's torment of her and her old friend **Terence Chang...**

They met over a decade ago. When the family first arrived from Hawaii. After...me.
When Victoria found herself drawn to Chinese opera, visiting almost weekly...
WHEN I DIDN'T SEE YOU LAST WEEK, I FIGURED SHE FINALLY GOT TIRED GAWKING--
THIS YOUNG LADY VENTURING INTO "DANGEROUS CHINAMEN TERRITORY"--
I'M NOT GAWKING.
AND THERE'S NOTHING DANGEROUS ABOUT THIS NEIGHBORHOOD. ANY IDIOT CAN SEE THAT.
Nevertheless, for the following weeks, Terence met her to ensure it.
And Victoria couldn't help growing close to this confident, optimistic man...
But it wasn't meant to be.
TERENCE, IT HAPPENS TO EVERYBODY...
"OUR LIVES DRIFTED APART-- UNTIL FRANKIE INTRODUCED HIM TO FATHER A LIFETIME LATER. TERENCE FOUND THE BEST CHINATOWN BUSINESSES TO INVEST IN--"

AND WE MET REGULARLY TO REVIEW THEM.
EVERYTHING FELT EASIER AROUND TERENCE. AND...WE FELL INTO OLD RHYTHMS. IT NEVER GREW... ROMANTIC. BUT...

But Woodward, who'd been shadowing her, mistook it for just that. Eventually he started following Terence...

"WHEN WOODWARD HANDED ME THOSE PHOTOS, IT ALL... MADE SENSE."

BUT THEN BENNIE SHOT WOODWARD, AND...WOODWARD BECAME DERANGED.
WHO KNOWS WHO HE'D COME AFTER NEXT? ME? FRANKIE? FATHER??

"OH, I PRETENDED TO BE FINE, BUT I'D STOPPED SLEEPING...
"AND WHEN IT SEEMED IVY KNEW HIS WHERE-ABOUTS...

"I INFORMED BENNIE AND DONNIE AND GAVE THEM ACCESS TO MR. NASH--WHO FATHER USED FOR... OFF-THE-BOOK ENDEAVORS. HE WAS SUPPOSED TO SCARE IVY, NOT--"
ARE YOU INSANE??

ARE *WE--? YOU* SAID IVY COULDN'T KNOW YOU'RE A *PART* OF THIS--
NASH IS *TORTURING* HER--!
SHE *KNOWS* WHERE WOODWARD IS, VICTORIA! SHE PRACTICALLY ADMITTED IT!

Maybe Ivy'd have lived if she hadn't fought so hard.
YOU WATCHED HER DIE TO PROTECT SOME FAIRY??
IT WOULDN'T HAVE JUST RUINED HIM--ALL HIS WORK IN CHINATOWN TOO--ALL BECAUSE WOODWARD WAS FOLLOWING ME!
SO YOU RISKED EVERYTHING JUST TO PROTECT MASON'S PET PROJECT--?
YOU IDIOT. DO YOU THINK FATHER EVER POURED THIS MUCH MONEY INTO ANYTHING?
THIS WASN'T MASON'S "PET PROJECT."
IT WAS MINE.
...
WHY THE HELL WOULD YOU CARE THAT MUCH?
YOU GODDAMN...
...YOU REALLY NEVER GOT IT, DID YOU?
WHAT'S WITH YOUR--
DON'T--

VICTORIA, WHAT DID YOU *DO?*

IT'S NOT... I WAS JUST--

JUST--

IT'S ALL *RIGHT,* DEAR.

I'LL HANDLE THINGS FROM HERE.

EDISON, VICTORIA HAS A *PLANE* TO CATCH TOMORROW.

YOU WORK AT SAL'S, HUH?
FUNNY. MY BOSS HAS A CRUSH ON A WAITRESS THERE. SOME THIN GIRL...
2 DAYS AGO
YOUR BOSS HAS A CRUSH ON RUBY?? SHE'S SO...AWKWARD.
WELL, THAT'S DEFINITELY HIS TYPE.
ANYTHING YOU COULD TELL ME ABOUT HER TO HELP ME SCORE POINTS WITH HIM--
WELL, I'LL SAY ONE THING--DON'T LET HER SEE YOU. SHE HATES US CHINESE.
E FOOD
SHE'S SEEN ME TAKING OUT THE TRASH, AND...Heh. SHE'S SO SCARED OF ME.
REALLY?
WELL, THAT'S GOOD TO KNOW, THANKS.
HEY, I APPRECIATE YOUR HELP.
I MEAN, SOME PUNK PUNCTURING MY TIRES IS ONE THING, BUT LOOK WHAT HE DID TO MY BASKET!!
IF YOU HADN'T COME ALONG, I COULDN'T HAVE GOTTEN MY GROCERIES HOME...

And as a broken Victoria slept, Mason explained--

"IVY DESCRIBED HERSELF AS AN ***OVERLOOKED*** CHILD. THIS 'HUI LONG' WAS JUST A YOUNG GIRL IMAGINING HOW TO ***CAPTIVATE*** CHINATOWN.

"SHE EVEN INVENTED THE ***FLOURISH*** OF REMOVING A VICTIM'S EYES, BECAUSE ALL TONG LEGENDS ***NEEDED*** EXTRAVAGANT TOUCHES.

"BUT WHEN HUI LONG'S ***FIRST*** VICTIM WAS REPORTED TO HAVE THE ***SAME*** FLOURISH IVY ***INVENTED,*** SHE WAS ***UNDERSTANDABLY*** UNSETTLED. AND THE ***ONLY*** PEOPLE SHE TOLD THOSE STORIES ***TO--***

"WERE HER FRIEND HOLLY...AND HER ***BROTHER.***

"WHICH, OF COURSE, ***INTENSIFIED*** HER WORRY.

"YOU SEE, ***MONTHS*** PRIOR, WOODWARD INFORMED HER HE'D COME INTO HIS ***FORTUNE***. SHE COULD QUIT HER JOB AND BE WITH ANYONE SHE DESIRED NOW.

"HOWEVER, WHEN IVY NOW INQUIRED ABOUT HER BROTHER, SHE COULDN'T ***LOCATE*** HIM. SHE RECALLED A JADE CASTLE STAMP ON HIS HAND DURING THEIR PREVIOUS ENCOUNTER.

"UNFORTUNATELY, THAT ***TOO*** PROVED A DEAD END.

"WHICH LED HER TO RECALL HOW HER INTEREST IN HUI LONG STEMMED FROM ***STORIES*** TOLD BY AN OLD NEIGHBOR. SO SHE RETURNED TO THE BUILDING SHE GREW UP IN.

"BUT SPEAKING TO ***HIM*** PROVED FRUITLESS AS WELL.

"LISTLESS NOSTALGIA BROUGHT HER BACK TO THE ***MAHJONG PARLOR*** WHERE HER MOTHER ONCE WORKED--TO DISCOVER ***EVERYONE*** TALKING ABOUT HUI LONG."

"WHICH LED IVY TO GROW FEARFUL...AND, WELL--***OBSESSED.*** I ***BEGGED*** HER TO FORGET IT..."

HOWEVER IT WAS CONNECTED TO HER BROTHER--SHE WAS INVESTIGATING A HATCHETMAN!
WE FOUGHT--AND THE NEXT DAY...I THOUGHT SHE RAN OFF, HOWEVER...
I CAN IMAGINE HOW VENGEFUL YOU MUST FEEL.
BUT SENDING NASH AFTER YOU...IT BROKE POOR VICTORIA. WE'RE FLYING HER TO SEE SOME DOCTORS IN EUROPE COME THE MORNING.
AND THEN IT'S OVER. I SWEAR. I'LL STAY THERE WITH HER. WE'LL BOTH NEVER RETURN--
WHO KILLED MY MOTHER, MASON?
WHAT--?
YOU-- YOU KNOW WHO--
DO I?

A WHILE BACK, I RESPONDED TO A MURDER. SOME BRUISER CRACKED HIS OLD LADY'S HEAD. BUT WHAT REALLY GOT ME WAS THE BROOCH AROUND HER NECK.
IT WAS ONE OF A KIND--AND STOLEN FROM YOUR MANSION THE NIGHT MA WAS MURDERED.
TURNS OUT, THAT WIFEBEATER TOOK IT.
'CUZ THE SAP WHO HUNG FOR THE CRIME--MICHAEL MARTINEZ--WAS INNOCENT. GOING THROUGH OLD REPORTS...IT WAS SO OBVIOUS.
YOU PUT THE FUZZ UNDER SO MUCH HEAT THEY PINNED IT ON SOME LOCAL WITH A RAP SHEET.
EXCEPT... THEY COULDN'T JUST HAND YOU A PATSY. YOU'RE TOO CONNECTED...
UNLESS YOU KNEW THAT'D BE THE BEST YOU'D GET. 'CUZ YOU MADE A PROMISE TO YOUR BOY. 'CUZ YOU'D DO ANYTHING FOR THOSE CLOSEST TO YOU, RIGHT?
WHAT... DOES ANY OF THIS--
MASON...

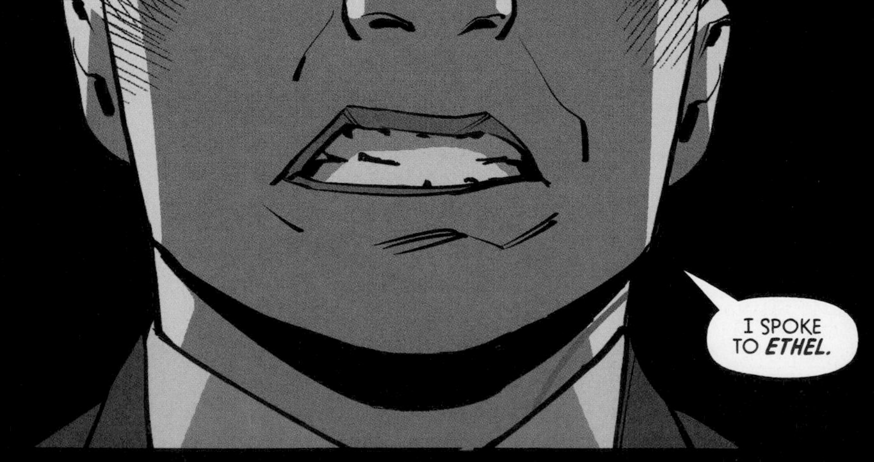
I SPOKE TO ETHEL.

YESTERDAY
WELL, IT'S ABOUT *TIME* MR. NEIGHBOR ASKED YOU OUT!
IT'S JUS'--JUS' A MOVIE...
OH, HE WOULDN'T ALWAYS BE CALLIN' IF HE WASN'T SWEET ON YA.
ANYWAY, YOU *SURE* YOU'RE GOOD TO LOCK UP?
YEAH... YOU HAVE A G'NITE.
ABYSSINIA, DOLL!
ABY--
SEEING YA--
KINK
KRSH
SHIT!
SHIT SHIT SHIT
HELLO?
OH--UM, SORRY. WE'RE-- WE'RE CLOSIN' SOON, BUT...
HEY, *ETHEL.*
OR I GUESS YOU PREFER *RUBY* NOW, HUH?

WHY DON'T YOU TELL ME WHAT HAPPENED IN SAN FRANCISCO?

MASON, VICTORIA TOLD ME YOU WERE MAKING WITHDRAWALS EVERY THIRD OF THE MONTH...
EVERY THIRD.
SAME DATE MA DIED.
BECAUSE THAT DATE--AND THE GUILT ASSOCIATED WITH IT--WAS SOMETHING YOU COULDN'T SHAKE, WAS IT?
AND WHATEVER IT WAS MAKING YOU DO...NOW THAT YOU'D WOKEN UP--I WONDERED--WERE YOU STILL DOING IT?
AND OF COURSE, YOU WERE. THAT DAY, ONLY ONE BIRD NOT DRESSED IN A FANCY SUIT CAME KNOCKING. I'M GUESSING A FRIEND WHO OWED YOU A FAVOR, RIGHT?
SO I FOLLOWED HIM. WATCHED HIM HAND AN ENVELOPE TO A GIRL WHO USED TO BE ETHEL--
A VAGRANT SECRETLY LIVING IN THAT WAREHOUSE WHERE IVY WAS MURDERED. AN EYEWITNESS WHO COULD IMPLICATE VICTORIA.
WHEN I GOT HERE, FRANKIE SAID YOU HIRED PINKERTONS TO FIND IVY--BUT THEY ONLY PRETENDED TO COME UP EMPTY, RIGHT?
I'M GUESSING THEY FOUND ETHEL, AND AFTER YOU HEARD THE TRUTH, YOU PAID HER OFF TO SKIP TOWN.
AND KEPT THE TAB RUNNING TO KEEP HER GONE.
FRANKIE'D NO IDEA IVY'S TRAIL WAS THE LAST THING YOU WANTED LOOKING INTO.
YOUR DAUGHTER KILLED THE WOMAN YOU LOVED, AND YOU COVERED IT UP.
AND THE WEIGHT OF IT CAUSED A HEART ATTACK.

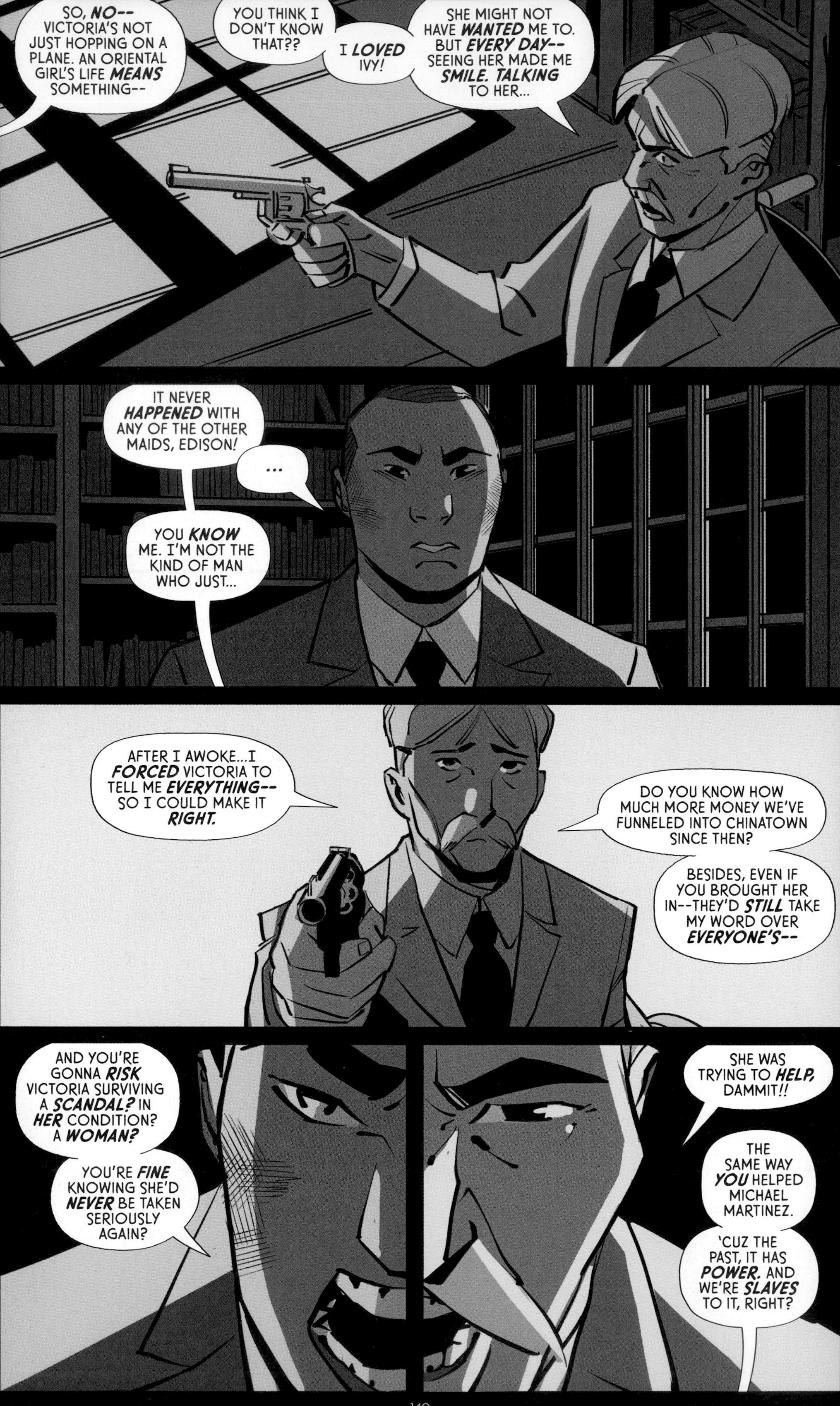
SO, NO-- VICTORIA'S NOT JUST HOPPING ON A PLANE. AN ORIENTAL GIRL'S LIFE MEANS SOMETHING--
YOU THINK I DON'T KNOW THAT??
I LOVED IVY!
SHE MIGHT NOT HAVE WANTED ME TO. BUT EVERY DAY-- SEEING HER MADE ME SMILE. TALKING TO HER...
IT NEVER HAPPENED WITH ANY OF THE OTHER MAIDS, EDISON!
...
YOU KNOW ME. I'M NOT THE KIND OF MAN WHO JUST...
AFTER I AWOKE...I FORCED VICTORIA TO TELL ME EVERYTHING-- SO I COULD MAKE IT RIGHT.
DO YOU KNOW HOW MUCH MORE MONEY WE'VE FUNNELED INTO CHINATOWN SINCE THEN?
BESIDES, EVEN IF YOU BROUGHT HER IN--THEY'D STILL TAKE MY WORD OVER EVERYONE'S--
AND YOU'RE GONNA RISK VICTORIA SURVIVING A SCANDAL? IN HER CONDITION? A WOMAN?
YOU'RE FINE KNOWING SHE'D NEVER BE TAKEN SERIOUSLY AGAIN?
SHE WAS TRYING TO HELP, DAMMIT!!
THE SAME WAY YOU HELPED MICHAEL MARTINEZ.
'CUZ THE PAST, IT HAS POWER. AND WE'RE SLAVES TO IT, RIGHT?

YOU WERE JUST A BOY, IT--IT WASN'T FAIR--
SO A MAN HUNG, SO A BOY COULD BELIEVE THE WORLD WAS...
A dream so pretty that when Victoria suggested a bigger mystery behind Ma's death... I jumped at it.

BUT REALLY, YOU JUST COULDN'T HANDLE THERE WAS NOTHING YOUR MILLIONS COULD DO TO MAKE THINGS BETTER--

SO WHAT'S YOUR ANSWER THEN?
I SHOULD HAVE JUST LET YOU SUFFER? VICTORIA SHOULD HAVE DONE NOTHING??

NOTHING WE'VE DONE SINCE MAKES ANY DIFFERENCE?

DAMMIT...

EDISON... ALL THIS HAS ALREADY COST ME THE WOMAN I LOVE...

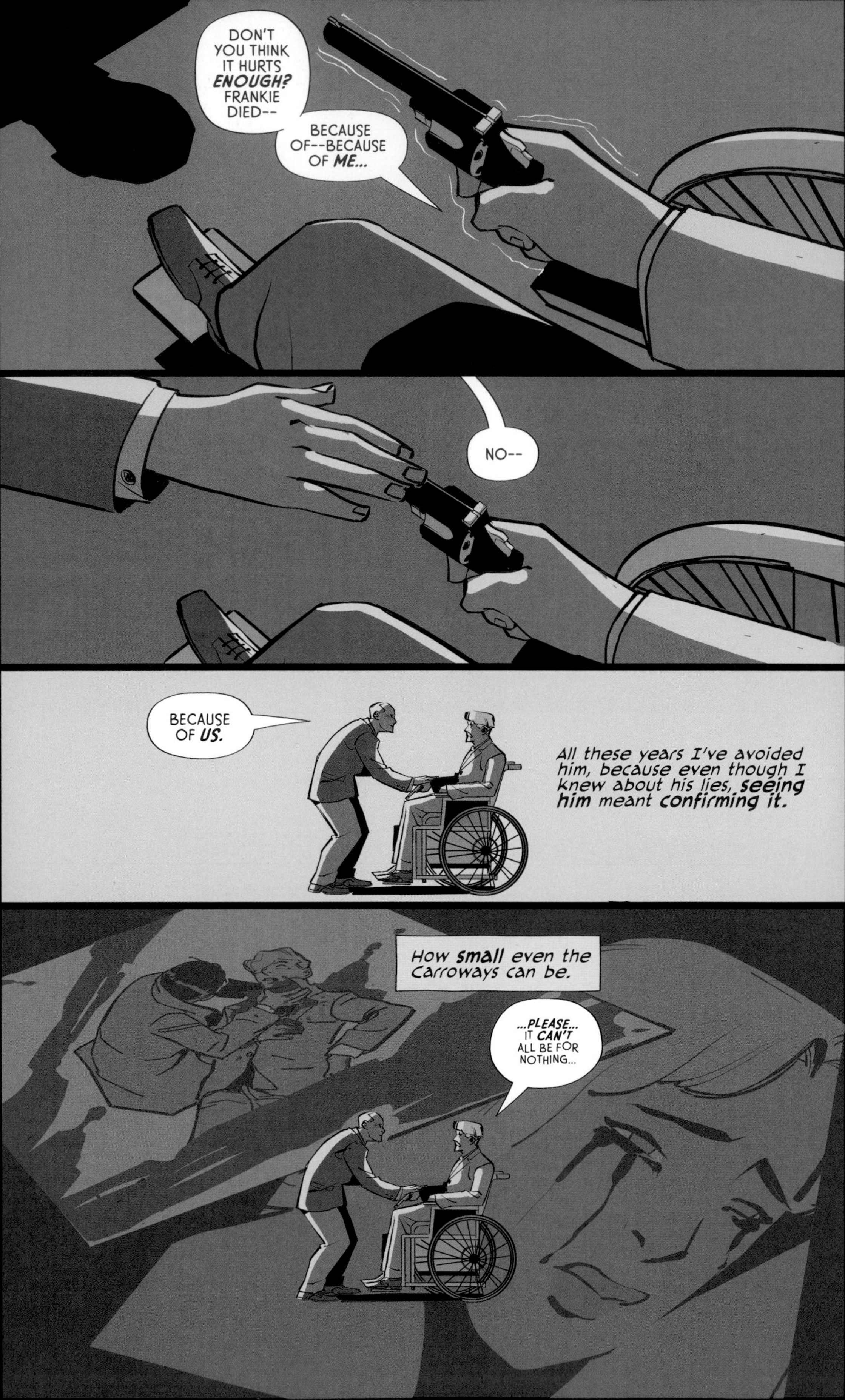

DON'T YOU THINK IT HURTS ***ENOUGH?*** FRANKIE DIED--

BECAUSE OF--BECAUSE OF ***ME...***

NO--

How ***small*** *even the Carroways can be.*

...PLEASE... IT ***CAN'T*** ALL BE FOR NOTHING...

...So we settle on the only option I *can* live with.
HERE. SIGNED CONFESSIONS OF EVERYTHING MASON AND VICTORIA DID.
AND TESTIMONIES TO EVERY OTHER SHADY TRANSACTION HIS COMPANY'S INVOLVED IN.
MASON AGREED TO HAND THEM OVER IN EXCHANGE FOR OUR TIGHT LIPS. HE ALSO DOUBLED HIS DONATIONS INTO CHINATOWN.
OH...MY GOD...
AFTER A FEW MONTHS, HE'LL BE BACK IN SAN FRANCISCO PERMANENTLY-- TO ENSURE REGARDLESS OF ANY FUTURE COMPROMISES, HIS MONEY NEVER STOPS FLOWING INTO CHINATOWN.
OR ELSE YOU'LL SECRETLY RELEASE THESE TO THE PAPERS AND RUIN HIM.
MAYBE THAT'LL BALANCE THE DAMAGE FRANKIE'S DEATH DID.
EDISON...I--I'M A SWITCHBOARD OPERATOR--
YEAH. IN CHINATOWN. WHICH MEANS YOU'RE ALWAYS LISTENING TO IT.
MAYBE THAT'S THE ONLY THING THAT CAN REALLY MAKE A DIFFERENCE.
'CUZ IF ANYONE'LL KNOW WHAT TO DO WITH THIS WHEN THE TIME'S RIGHT...

IT'S *YOU.*

JESUS. ***OK,*** BUT...
YOU'RE JUST-- ***LEAVING?***

EVEN IF FOLKS DON'T RECOGNIZE ME, EVERYONE ***STILL*** THINKS EDISON HARK KILLED FRANKIE CARROWAY.
BUS Lines
TRIP PASS-
Mr.
Pass
SUBJECT TO
From
AUG
SEPT
OCT

AND THIS FACE I'M STILL ***ADJUSTING*** TO DOESN'T HAVE A BADGE TO ***HIDE*** BEHIND ANYMORE.
BUT...
SORRY...

I'M JUST GETTING THE WORD OUT ABOUT THE COMMUNITY MEETING TONIGHT.
!

WE'RE BRAINSTORMING WHAT WE ***ALL*** CAN DO TO MAKE AMERICANS COMFORTABLE IN CHINATOWN AGAIN...
*Of **course**, I'd see Terence Chang again...*

Look *at him. We almost ruined his* ***life.*** *He* ***must*** *think whoever orchestrated him seeing Victoria that night is still out there...*

But he's still going.
...BECAUSE REAL CHANGE MEANS GETTING AMERICANS TO FORGET ALL THIS!
WE NEED AMERICANS TO SEE US AS ANYTHING BUT THREATS.
AND THAT'S IT?
THE ANSWER'S JUST... CONTORTING OURSELVES FOR THE GWEILOS' CHARITY?
WELL, HOW MUCH WILL THINGS CHANGE WITHOUT IT?
SURE, BUT AT WHAT COST?
HIDING AND ACTING LIKE WHO WE REALLY ARE IS SOMETHING TO BE ASHAMED OF? YOU BELIEVE THAT?
...
SIGH
YOU WANT TO KNOW WHAT I BELIEVE?
WHAT I REALLY THINK WHEN I THINK OF ALL THIS?

"I THINK OF CHOP SUEY.
"IT'S MADE AT EVERY CHINATOWN RESTAURANT, AND IT'S THE FIRST THING AMERICANS ORDER.
"THEY'VE NO IDEA CHOP SUEY'S NOT FROM CHINA.
"THEY DON'T KNOW IT WAS INVENTED--HERE IN CHINATOWN--TO MAKE CHINESE FOOD--TO MAKE CHINESE PEOPLE--SEEM LESS THREATENING.
"AND TO AN EXTENT, IT WORKED. AMERICANS BECAME COMFORTABLE WITH IT, EVEN THOUGH IT'S NEITHER CHINESE NOR AMERICAN...
"IT'S SOMETHING NEW.
"MADE FROM THE CIRCUMSTANCES IT TOOK TO SURVIVE.
"AND NOW AMERICA ASSUMES IT WAS ALWAYS THERE."

"BECAUSE I DON'T THINK WE'LL ***EVER*** BE ONE OF THEM. NOT REALLY.

"WE'RE SOMETHING ***NEW.*** SOMETHING ***ELSE.*** WE JUST NEED TIME TO ***DEFINE*** IT."

JESUS, O'MALLEY, IF YOU GOTTA DRINK--

"TO LEARN HOW TO ***FIGHT*** FOR IT.

"BECAUSE ***NOTHING'S*** MORE AMERICAN THAN FIGHTING FOR SOMETHING ***NEW."***

DON'T LET THE DAMN LOCALS SEE YA...

This all started 'cuz of Ivy Chen...

The girl I was sent here to find. The girl who ***died*** *before I* ***could.***

*I asked Mason who she was--****really****--and he described someone looking to start over. A person who* ***regretted*** *her mistakes.*

Not at all the ***seductress*** *those men in her mother's mahjong parlor told me about--*

Or the ***victim*** *Victoria described--*

Or the ***manipulator*** *Holly Chao resented--*

Or the ***saint*** *Silas Woodward worshipped--*

Were ***any*** *of them right? Or was Ivy just...*

Another Oriental
trying to **survive.**

Because sometimes
survival's just **hiding--**
so **you** can't be used
against you.

And like **anything**
staying hidden for too
long, it risks getting **lost.**

Because who are we?

Beyond the work we
take on and the legacies
we inherit?

In that space between
our obligation to
ourselves and our
people...

What's **left?**

Who **are** we?

IN 1943, AMERICA-- LOOKING TO CHINA AS AN ALLY AGAINST WARRING JAPAN-- LIFTED THE CHINESE EXCLUSION ACT.

THE NUMBER OF CHINESE ALLOWED TO ENTER THE COUNTRY WAS FINALLY EXPANDED...

...TO NO MORE THAN ONE HUNDRED AND FIVE IMMIGRANTS A YEAR.

...NOT A ONE.

OTHER LAWS WOULD
CONTINUE RESTRICTING
ASIANS AND ARABS FROM
ENTERING AMERICA
UNTIL THE IMMIGRATION
AND NATIONALITY ACT
OF 1965.

EDISON HARK WILL RETURN.

— *Fin* —

THE GOOD ASIAN

HISTORICAL NOTES

HARK'S REAL-LIFE INSPIRATION

While Hark's psyche and conflicts are my creation and interpretation, I've clung very closely to precedent in crafting his history, liberally stealing from the life of America's first Chinese detective **– Chang Apana,** who preceded Hark by decades and also served as the inspiration for the 20th century's most famous Asian detective – Charlie Chan.

A recount of Chang Apana's life could easily be criticized as "too comic book-y." He started off as a Hawaiian cowboy, regularly carrying a bullwhip, even as a cop. He was generally considered a master of disguise. He had a scar over his eye given to him by a Japanese leper who attacked him with a sickle. Drug addicts once threw him out of a second story window, only for him to land on his feet and run back in to arrest them. Once, while casing out a suspicious cargo ship, he was run over by a horse and buggy. Another time –without back-up and armed only with his whip – he arrested forty gamblers who he single-handedly lined up and marched to the police station.

These incredible exploits aside... Detective Chang Apana was born on December 26, 1871 in the village of Waipio, his first name a Hawaiianized version of the Chinese name Ah Pung (Chinese names typically listed as [last name] [first name]). While his parents came to Hawaii as laborers, lack of work and homesickness found them returning to China when Chang was only three. But the Opium Wars and the Taiping Revolution had devastated their rural Canton, plunging their home into poverty. And so, when Chang was ten, his parents had him accompany his uncle back to Hawaii, hoping he'd fare better in America than they had.

Chang would eventually become a *paniolo* – a Hawaiian cowboy. Helen Kinau Wilder – the owner of Chang's horses and a champion of social reform – was so impressed she hired him to be an animal case investigator for the newly founded Hawaiian chapter of the Humane Society. While the job only involved investigating animal cruelty, because the Society was technically part of the Honolulu Police Department, it was a position Chang could never have attained without the patronage of the rich white Wilder.

A friend of Wilder's – a Hawaiian Marshall – was likewise impressed by Chang, hiring him to be an officer in the police force. In 1898, Chang became America's first Chinese-American police officer. As part of the Honolulu PD, one of Chang's responsibilities involved arresting Chinese lepers, so they could be deported to the leper colony on the island of Molokai, leprosy at the time considered a "Chinese disease."

Chang also became invaluable during sting operations, becoming one of Hawaii's first undercover cops, since one of the major vices the police were charged with cracking down on was gambling – a favorite pastime for many Chinese.

Chang's most common undercover disguise was posing as a See Yup Man. See Yup Men are Chinese street peddlers dangling two baskets of goods on either end of a shoulder pole. Chang would enter gambling dens pretending to sell goods but actually peeking at the operation so he could tell the raiding cops what to look out for.

Eventually, Chang's considerable exploits received newspaper attention. While the writer Earl Derr Biggers was doing research for his novel *The House Without a Key*, he read of Chang's exploits and inserted a Chinese detective character a quarter way into his novel. That character stole the show, and Biggers' next novel, *The Chinese Parrot,* started a series of books centering around the adventures of Charlie Chan. Biggers eventually met Chang in 1928, giving him credit for inspiring his famous Asian detective. Four years later, Chang retired from active duty after being injured in a car accident.

For more information on either Detective Chang Apana or Charlie Chan, check out *Charlie Chan: The Untold Story of the Honorable Detective and His Rendezvous with American History* by Yunte Huang.

THE MASSIE TRIAL

Wilbur Manalao's story is very much inspired by the considerably more explosive Massie trial, one of the most infamous and important legal cases of 1930s Hawaii.

By the 1930s, Hawaii was a playground for wealthy Americans. While the island's overwhelming majority was nonwhite, including its entire low-paid workforce, a small, wealthy white minority — who locals referred to as haoles — controlled the economy, living lives of opulence.

Thalia Fortescue Massie was a 20-year-old wife of a rising US Navy officer stationed there. She also hailed from an affluent family, being a descendant to inventor Alexander Graham Bell. On September 12, 1931, she was found one night wandering a deserted Honolulu road, having been beaten, her jaw broken. She claimed to have been abducted while leaving a nearby nightclub, and when questioned, stated a group of Hawaiian men had assaulted and robbed her. While initially she said it was too dark to provide details on the men or their car, hours later, she reported to police not only had she had been raped, but described her assailants as "locals," able to recite their license plate number.

Within hours, the police arrested the alleged assailants. Two were of Hawaiian ancestry, two were Japanese, and one was half-Chinese / half-Hawaiian. And while Massie's story initially seemed credible, it proceeded to fall apart. It was later unearthed that officers taking her statement had fed her information, including the license plate number of the five accused. Additionally, there was no evidence Massie had been raped, while records showed the alleged attackers were involved in a car accident across town around the time of Massie's assault.

Numerous rumors and theories circulated about what really happened that night. Some alleged Massie had not been raped at all. Others believed she was having an affair with one of her alleged attackers. Another theory involved Massie cheating on her husband with one of his friends, it being her husband who broke her jaw upon discovering the infidelity.

These claims enraged Massie's mother, **Grace Fortescue**, who saw them as smears against her family's good name, starting a public campaign to attack the defendants. But due to lack of evidence and conflicting testimony, the case fell apart. After a three-week trial — the court's spectators' gallery frequently jam-packed with an audience — the case against the accused ended with a hung jury mistrial.

According to one account of the proceedings, "bedlam broke loose in the halls of the judiciary building following the discharge of the jury." Some in the Navy viewed the failure to convict the attackers of a Naval wife as publicly shaming their forces. Given that Hawaii prohibited juries to be comprised exclusively of people from only one race, they believed the accused were let go because of racial solidarity. Local paper *The Honolulu Times* covered the events under the headline "The Shame of Honolulu." And while Hawaiians considered the paper a sensationalistic tabloid, the publication eventually circulated to the mainland, influencing the trial's coverage in national news.

In the spring of 1932, *The New York Times* ran almost two hundred stories about the events surrounding the Massie trial. The case was voted by Associated Press editors as one of the top news events of the year — and the most important criminal trial in the country. The Honolulu Citizen's Organization for Good Government was formed with a list of demands including "the sterilization of certain delinquents." The story so dominated mainland America, movie theaters opened their programs with news footage of the ongoing "native uprising" in the islands. *Time Magazine* published a story headlined "Lust in Paradise," describing the islands' "motley population" and the rape of "the daughter of a gallant soldier, the granddaughter of one of the world's greatest inventors," describing how in this "paradise melting pot of East & West... yellow men's lust for white women had broken bounds."

In contrast to mainland hysteria, however, there was in fact no record of a Hawaiian ever raping a *haole* woman by the time of the trial, although there was a history going back centuries of *haoles* raping Hawaiians. Most of these men, if captured, pleaded to reduced charges and received little punishment. In fact, *The New York Times*'s Pulitzer Prize-winning Russell Owen had once been told by one of Honolulu's prominent businessmen that "when he was a boy, attending the exclusive school for white children in Honolulu, he and some of his friends used to find it lots of fun to take some Hawaiian girl out on a dark road at night and rape her."

Massie's mother, Grace Fortescue, became obsessed with getting the accused men jailed pending a second trial. But without new solid evidence, she was told there was no chance of a conviction. Incensed, Fortescue arranged for the kidnapping and vicious beating of one of the accused. Then, she enlisted Massie's husband and two other Navy men to kidnap another plaintiff — **Joseph Kahahawai** — the darkest skinned of the five defendants. The four attempted to beat a confession out of him, ending with one of them shooting and killing Kahahawai.

While they were attempting to dump the body, a passing policeman noted suspicious activity, pulling them over and discovered Kahahawai. The officer immediately arrested all four.

Fortescue and her colleagues were now on trial for murder. For her defense, the socialite hired no less than Clarence Darrow, leading member of the ACLU, bringing the lawyer famous for his involvement in the Leopold and Loeb murder trial out of retirement.

Believing Fortescue and her navy accomplices would not be safe in a jail containing Hawaiian guards and prisoners, the four were imprisoned in a decommissioned ship in permanent dry dock at Pearl Harbor. *Time Magazine* described Fortescue's quarters as a "penthouse, bristling with ventilators to cool the neat single cabins within, each comparable to that on a small liner." With staterooms for cells, the accused murderers of Joseph Kahahawai had "books, cards, and music... electric fans, call bells, and all the conveniences of a modern hotel." The onboard officer's mess hall provided their meals. The four also became overwhelmed with flower deliveries, well-wishers who saw Fortescue as a celebrity wrongly punished for defending her daughter's honor.

Meanwhile, fearing more violence against the remaining four men charged but found not guilty of attacking Thalia Massie, the four were taken in for protective custody, locked up for their own security at Honolulu's municipal jail. If they wanted to eat, their families and friends had to provide the food.

No one in Honolulu wanted to serve in the jury of the trial of Grace Fortescue, fearing they'd

inevitably offend someone whichever way they voted. When the trial inevitably did happen, Fortescue and her colleagues were ultimately charged with manslaughter (rather than murder) for the death of Joseph Kahahawai.

The mainland press exploded. Every Hearst newspaper condemned the "Hawaiian rabble" and provided a form for readers to fill out and mail to their representatives urging them "to take immediate action to afford the protection of the United States government to American women in Hawaii... and to force respect in Hawaii for the American flag and its defenders." The volume of mail and cable messages out of Washington, D.C. on the topic was greater than on any subject since the end of World War I.

Meanwhile, members of Congress began calling upon President Hoover to pardon Fortescue and her colleagues. Senators and congressmen lined up to introduce a flood of legislation designed to punish Hawaii. At one point, martial law was even suggested if rioting were to begin.

At a certain point, the Governor hired the Pinkerton's National Detective Agency to further investigate Thaila Massie's attack. They responded with a 279-page report, citing their investigation "makes it impossible to escape the conviction that the kidnapping and assault was not caused by those accused." The White House, however, pressured Hawaii's governor to suppress the report, fearing embarrassment if the five innocent men who had been arrested and tried – one even murdered – were found innocent for a rape that never occurred.

Under pressure from the Navy, Fortescue and her colleagues' ten-year sentences were commuted to one hour served in the high sheriff's office. Days later, the four convicted killers and Thalia Massie boarded a ship back to the mainland, leaving Hawaii as national celebrities.

But the Massie trial would prove a pivotal moment in Hawaii's racial reckoning. The events would lead Hawaiian, Japanese, Chinese, and Filipino community leaders to begin meeting and finding common ground. Meanwhile, prominent *haole* residents in the legal community, press, and politics, abhorred by the events, began speaking out against the arrogance of the long-standing *haole* oligarchy. The combined efforts would start a shift in racial attitudes, and eventually, the politics and laws of the land followed.

For more on the Massie trial, check out *Honor Killing: Race, Rape, and Clarence Darrow's Spectacular Last Case* by David E. Stannard.

THE GOOD ASIAN PROPOSAL

The following is the original proposal sent to Image Comics leading to the greenlight of the series. It is presented here in its original entirety, although much of the story would end up changing in the writing — most significantly, the names of almost all the characters.

THE GOOD ASIAN

(A 10-issue series written by Pornsak Pichetshote with art by Alexandre Tefenkgi; colors by TBD; letters & design by Jeff Powell; edited by Will Dennis)

THE LOGLINE: Following a Chinese-American detective on the trail of a killer in 1936 Chinatown, THE GOOD ASIAN is Asian film noir starring the first generation of Americans to come of age under an immigration ban… the Chinese.

THE CONCEPT: **EDISON HARK (33)** is a burnt-out Chinese-American detective who's built his career on turning in Chinese criminals in his native Hawaii. But when the hunt for a missing person leads him to San Francisco's Chinatown district – where a series of killings threaten to derail the repeal of the Chinese Exclusion Act (the immigration ban prohibiting the Chinese from entering America since 1882) – his investigation will force him to re-examine everything he cherishes, in a murder mystery asking how much obligation we have to our race.

THE PROTAGONIST: After his mother died, young **EDISON HARK** was taken in by her rich, white employer and raised as one of his own. That upbringing imparted him with an appreciation for the law, while a lifetime assimilating in a white world gave Hark an almost Sherlock Holmes-ian ability to read people. The insight would make him a masterful detective. But the department found the best use for him as an undercover officer, infiltrating Chinese opium and gambling dens and turning in perpetrators. While he justified his actions by believing they were for the greater good, a career of turning in his own people has left Hark broken and cynical, believing the Chinese will always be second-class citizens in America. Burnt-out and cynical, Hark is an undercover cop who's become such a good liar, he too easily fools himself.

THE APPEAL: THE GOOD ASIAN is set in an era never before explored in fiction – when America banned Chinese immigrants. Exploring immigration bans, police brutality, and identity politics, the book flips mystery tropes on its head to tells a story about Asian-American identity, all while introducing a tough, sexy, yet deeply conflicted male Asian protagonist. In a post-*Crazy Rich Asians* world, the book explores events unique to the Chinese-American perspective such as **Angel Island,** the immigration center / concentration camp Chinese immigrants were kept before they could enter America; **paper sons,** the unique way the Chinese faked immigration papers; and the fascinatingly singular popularity of **Chop Suey nightclub circuit** in the 1930s.

THE CREATORS: PORNSAK PICHETSHOTE was a Thai-American editor at DC/VERTIGO, his books having been nominated for dozens of Eisners. His hit Image book INFIDEL earned spots on 20+ Best of the Year's lists, including *NPR*, *The Hollywood Reporter*, and *The Huffington Post*, while securing a film option within two issues. ALEXANDRE TEFENKGI is an international illustrator – the co-creator of Image's OUTPOST ZERO in America and *Where are the Great Days?* in France. JEFF POWELL has lettered comics for over two decades, including Kaare Andrews' RENATO JONES, INFIDEL, and the Eisner-nominated *Atomic Robo*. From Image's UNDISCOVERED COUNTRY and FAMILY TREE to DC/ Vertigo's *100 Bullets* and *Y: The Last Man*, WILL DENNIS is one of the most respected editors in comics. His work has been nominated for countless Eisners.

THE GOOD ASIAN condensed overview

The year is 1936. **Edison Hark** is a burnt-out Chinese-American police detective working in Hawaii. After a career as an undercover cop selling out his own people, he's come to accept no matter how much he tries to justify his actions, things will never get better; the Chinese will always be second-class citizens. He's called to San Francisco by his white surrogate family, the **Thurstons** – stern patriarch **George Thurston**, repentant eldest **Spencer Thurston**, and overachieving youngest **Victoria Thurston** – only to find George has taken ill. It was Spencer who summoned him to find **May Chen**, the family housekeeper and his father's secret love, Spencer hoping to reunite the two before the old man passes.

Looking for leads, Hark investigates San Francisco's Chinatown district where he finds a community terrorized by cops and yet still believing they're on the verge of acceptance; that America's ban on Chinese immigrants will soon be lifted. And while a younger, more idealistic Hark might have related, everything this cop has seen since has made him too jaded. But the more he uncovers about the missing May Chen, he discovers a ghost of his former self: A cynical woman who also discovered idealism working for the Thurstons. But in her case, was it just an act for their benefit? Answering that question takes on increasing significance as Hark discovers May's path is linked to a killer's – a fabled Tong boss named **Hui Long** – on the loose at a time when Washington is keeping careful watch on America's Chinatowns, as Congress votes to repeal the Chinese Exclusion Act.

As Hui Long's killings escalate, Hark finds himself continually two steps behind him – as he also meets a generation of Chinese-Americans who grew up during the immigration ban, people with a much different perspective on race than Hark had growing up in Hawaii. Despite being inspired by their stories, Hark will be continually forced to believe that the only way a Chinese cop can protect other Chinese is by selling them out. In the process, he'll meet **Terence Chang,** an Obama-esque lawyer rehabilitating Chinatown's public image (who Hark believes is corrupt) and become reacquainted with Victoria Thurston – who Hark dated in high school, their relationship a secret since miscegenation was illegal.

The tension builds when Hark must chase Hui Long with a stubborn Spencer in tow – the killer murdering him to escape. And Spencer's death isn't just disastrous for personal reasons. Realizing news of a dead white man in Chinatown would kill the repeal of the Chinese Exclusion Act, Hark covers up his killing… only to be caught red-handed and blamed for his death.

A fugitive on the run, Hark goes to the only person he can trust – Victoria Thurston. They overcome their considerable baggage to track down Hui Long, in the process unearthing his connection to May Chen: That Hui Long is a smokescreen used by May Chen's *white* half-brother **Raymond Gold**. Gold is using the Hui Long identity to cover his tracks as he murders a cadre of Chinatown VIPs. And in the process of discovering *that,* Victoria uncovers that May Chen is in fact alive and working with her blood-thirsty half-brother. The revelation disheartens a downtrodden Hark; he so desperately wants to believe a cynic could find optimism through the Thurstons like he once did, a part of him believing that perhaps his descent into cynicism was through losing touch with the values George Thurston imparted on him.

It culminates in an epic battle between Gold and Hark. The detective eventually wins, but not before Gold practically carves Hark's face open – grotesquely scarring him. But before Gold can confess his motive, he and Hark are both mowed down by an unseen GUNMAN.

Six months later, and the damage to Chinatown has been done. The repeal of the Exclusion Act has failed; Hark is believed to be Spencer Thurston's murderer; and George Thurston has miraculously recuperated. We reveal a slowly recuperating Hark, one with a new face due to plastic surgery. So disguised, he gets the drop on the Gunman who shot him, discovering the mastermind behind his shooting – and the last person Gold meant to kill – Victoria Thurston.

Confronting Victoria, Hark learns that she and Terence have been having a secret affair. But a year ago, Gold began blackmailing them with pictures. With miscegenation illegal, the revelation would have destroyed Terence's standing, negating his good work. Victoria and other influential Chinatown players planned to eliminate Gold. But the murder attempt failed, allowing him to escape. When Gold finally recuperated, he used the legend of Hui Long – one which his sister May Chen once told him – as a smokescreen to cover his killings. But spotting the erroneous remnants she incorrectly recalled of Hui Long legend in the killings, May Chen realized her estranged half-brother must be involved, leaving the Thurston home in search of him.

But if May Chen went looking for Hui Long, where is she now? Dead, sadly, as Hark eventually deduces Victoria lied about seeing her – because *Victoria* in fact killed her. She confesses: May Chen came to Victoria with the results of her search for her stepbrother, and Victoria, knowing the trail would eventually lead back to her, had May Chen killed, disposing of the body.

But upon learning this, George Thurston still won't allow Victoria to be arrested, vowing to use all his resources to move them out of San Francisco, away from the law. Because no matter her heinous crime, Victoria is still his daughter.

The story ends with Hark harshly realizing that as cynical as he is, he was still idolizing the Thurstons. But his interactions with Chinatown will lead him to an even more disappointing conclusion: that despite believing he chose being a cop as the lesser of two evils to protect his fellow Chinese, he's in fact lived his entire life secretly yearning to be accepted by whites.

With his new face, Hark encounters Terence one final time in the midst of the lawyer trying to gain white support to repeal the Chinese Exclusion Act, and Hark realizes his suspicions of Terence all stemmed from his jealousy of Terence's unshakeable idealism. And while Hark will try to impart what he's learned to Terence – that jockeying for white favor will never truly set the Chinese free – Terence will counter with a cold truth – they also have no hope of equality without it. Hearing the truth in Terence's words, Hark departs, acknowledging for the first time how much Chinatown needs a man like Terence.

But a man like him? Of that, he's less sure. Hark leaves Chinatown an outlaw, bereft of friends and family. But with a new face, a new life, finally his own man…

Curious if America has a place for that.

EDISON
HARK
THE GOOD ASIAN
1936

PORNSAK PICHETSHOTE was a Thai-American rising star editor at DC's VERTIGO imprint, his books nominated for dozens of Eisner awards. Currently writing for television and comics, his TV credits include *Marvel's Cloak & Dagger* and *Green Lantern* for HBO Max. His hit graphic novel INFIDEL was selected for NPR's "100 Favorite Horror Stories of All Time."

ALEXANDRE TEFENKGI is a French comic book artist of Vietnamese-Djiboutian descent. He started his career in the European market working with some of France's top publishers. His first international book is the critically acclaimed sci-fi series OUTPOST ZERO for Skybound Entertainment.

LEE LOUGHRIDGE is a devilishly handsome man, despite his low testosterone, who has been working primarily in the comics/animation industry for over twenty years. He has worked on hundreds of titles for all the industry's major publishers, his talents on display on every iconic comic book character from Batman to Punisher to DEADLY CLASS and more.

JEFF POWELL has lettered a wide range of titles throughout his lengthy career. His recent work includes *The Devil's Red Bride, Scales & Scoundrels,* and *The Forgotten Blade*. In addition, Jeff has designed books, logos, and trade dress for Marvel, Archie, IDW, Image, Valiant, and others.

DAVE JOHNSON may be best known for his minimalist covers on the noir Vertigo series, *100 Bullets*. He has also done a number of covers for Marvel, DC, and Image Comics. He earned the 2002 Eisner Award for Best Cover Artist and has also been nominated for an Eisner in 2004 and 2021. His work on the critically acclaimed *Superman: Red Son* is also a perennial bestseller.

WILL DENNIS was an editor at Vertigo/DC Entertainment for more than fifteen years, specializing in genre fiction comics and graphic novels. His award-winning titles include *100 Bullets, Y: The Last Man, Joker* and many more. He is currently a freelance editor for Image Comics, ComiXology, and DC Entertainment, also writing *The Art of Jock* for Insight Editions.